RIVERS
of
STONE

RIVERS
of
STONE

A Novel
ROBERT PRUITT

First Fiction Series

SANTA FE

All of the characters in this fictional story are themselves fictional,
and any similarity to persons living or dead
is purely coincidental.

Sketches by Mitch Tatafu

Sunstone books may be purchased for educational, business, or sales promotional
use. For information please write: Special Markets Department, Sunstone Press,
P.O. Box 2321, Santa Fe, New Mexico 87504-2321.

Library of Congress Cataloging-in-Publication Data:

Pruitt, Robert G.
    Rivers of stone: a novel / by Robert Pruitt.
        p. cm. -- (First fiction series)
    ISBN: 0-86534-347-0
    1. Diamond industry and trade—Fiction. 2. Navajo Indians—Fiction.
    3. Geologists—Fiction. 4. Utah—Fiction. I. Title. II. Series.

PS3616. R59 R48 2002
813'.6—dc21   2002022771

Published in

SUNSTONE PRESS
Post Office Box 2321
Santa Fe, NM 87504-2321 / USA
(505) 988-4418 / *orders only* (800) 243-5644
FAX (505) 988-1025
www.sunstonepress.com

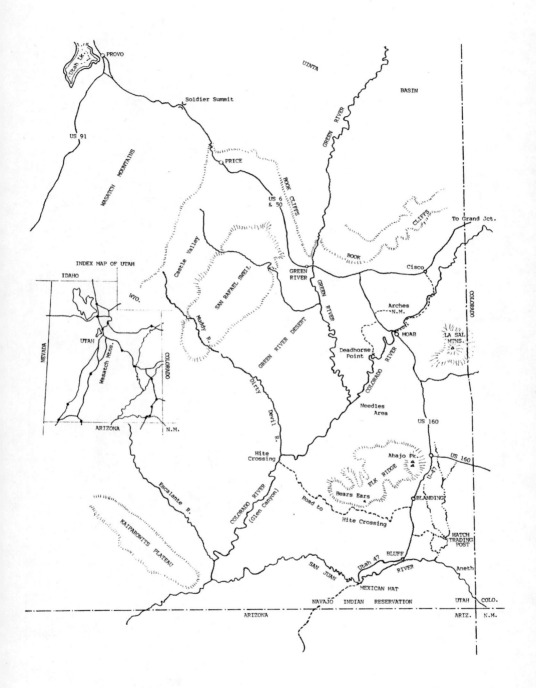

Partial Map of Utah Highways

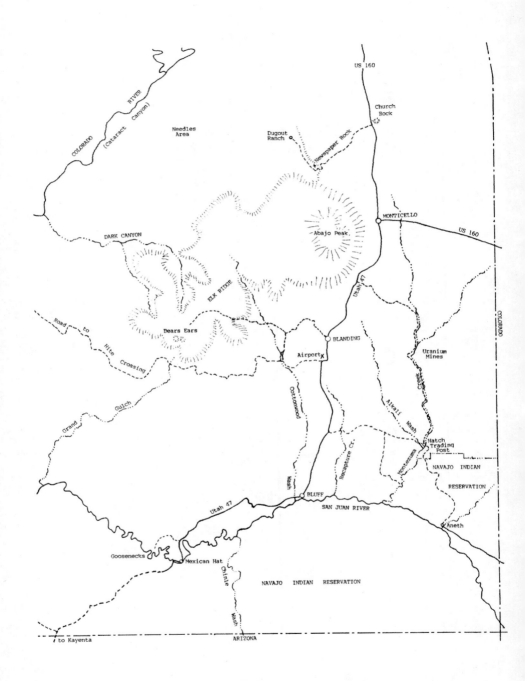

Southeastern Utah's Canyon Country

FORWARD

Over the past 200 million years the face of southeastern Utah has changed greatly, from Jurassic desert wastelands to Cretaceous swamps, to the present uplifted and eroded sandstone cliffs of modern Canyon Country, where preserved sedimentary layers representing virtually this entire time interval can be seen and studied.

The world we live in was formed long ago. The scenic grandeur we admire today is the result of eons of change, by geologic upheaval followed by the erosive forces of wind and water. Geology is the scholastic study of these earth-forming processes. An exploration geologist is one who is trained to find deposits of valuable minerals created by these geologic processes, but he is successful only if he can find economically recoverable concentrations of valuable minerals. The analogy of prospecting for minerals with a treasure hunt is not farfetched.

This adventure story tells how intelligent deduction, coupled with energetic persistence, can be used to unravel and decipher mysteries of the ancient past in the hope of creating new wealth where only desolation once existed. It takes place near the Navajo Indian Reservation in the southern Colorado Plateau Region of southeastern Utah during the late 1950s, at the time of the Uranium Boom following World War II and the Korean Conflict. Circumstances and people were somewhat different then, but the actual places retain their awesome beauty and much of their remoteness even today. Think back to the late 1950s and enjoy the adventure.

1

THE QUEST

A warm, gusting south wind made the tattered remnants of Christmas lights and decorations still hanging across downtown Salt Lake City's State Street rattle and dance on their moorings. It was a late winter evening in early March, and the strong south wind heralded an approaching cold front and its inevitable snow storm. As the tower clock in the 19th century Victorian style City and County Building completed chiming nine o'clock, the high pitched whine of a straining automobile engine could be heard in the distance. The extremely wide downtown streets of Salt Lake City were especially desolate on this dark Sunday evening, with dead leaves and the tatters of someone's newspaper racing before the gusting south wind.

A dark green 1954 Willys Jeep station wagon suddenly roared up State Street past the City and County Building and through the intersection of Fourth South with its traffic light dancing overhead in the wind. The boxy Jeep station wagon turned sharply left into a narrow side street between tall office buildings and pulled into a narrow alley. Its engine slowed and died as if in relief. The driver's door opened and a dusty figure clothed in khaki pants, khaki shirt and field boots slowly emerged and paused for a moment to get the kinks out after a long drive.

Clayton P. Greer, independent consulting geologist, had driven his under-powered field vehicle nonstop for the last twelve hours from Kanab in southern Utah all the way to Salt Lake City, over two lane highways that were outdated by even the standards of 1957. He fumbled with a ring of keys and unlocked the building side door, propping it open with a chunk of petrified wood lying nearby. He unlocked the rear of the station wagon and loaded a half dozen heavy canvas bags onto a small handcart he retrieved from behind the open door. Then he reached into the back of the station wagon and took out a shallow cardboard tray containing over two dozen smaller cotton bags with paper labels attached. He inspected them carefully, loaded them onto the cart and wheeled it into the building after locking the Jeep and closing the building door. Inside, he took the elevator and rode to the fourth floor and headed down the corridor to a glass paneled door marked:

Suite 418

Office of Clayton P. Greer

Consulting Geologist & Mine Valuations

He unlocked the door and entered. Parking the handcart next to a table in the front office, he stopped to sort the mail piled on the secretarial desk. The small office suite was sparsely furnished with oak desks, table and chairs, and a bright new IBM Selectric typewriter stood atop an ancient secretarial desk in the front office. A drab linoleum floor and a hanging fluorescent ceiling fixture completed the spartan decor. Painted wooden file cabinets and wooden plank wall shelves in both the outer and inner offices, even a metal bookcase in the rear office, were cluttered with rock specimens and mineral ores ranging in size from a large melon down to a walnut. The cast iron steam radiator under the single window in the rear office was capped with a plank, and it too was heavy with mineral specimens. The books on the shelves and in the bookcase were mostly thin paper-backed government publications with complex titles and a certain drabness that characterized the entire office. The small suite looked more like a workroom than a professional office.

Clayton Greer was a slender, stooped young man in his mid-30s, of medium height and trim build, with short dark blond hair and a ruddy complexion. His khaki clothing made him look like a military man, but a very casual one. His bright intelligent eyes and confident facial expression bespoke a professionalism that contrasted with the drab office furnishings. There was no wasted motion as he quickly went through the mail, discarding junk mail, holding envelopes containing checks up to the ceiling light, and opening a few envelopes containing correspondence. He glanced at a note pad next to the rotary telephone, then went to the rear office and spotted a typed note taped to the back of his chair where he couldn't miss it. It read:

Clay—

> PLEASE call Mr. George (sounds like a new client) at the Newhouse Hotel as soon as you arrive Sunday, even if it is late.
>
> Jeanie

Clay looked at his watch. It was now 9:25. He paused, then picked up the telephone and dialed a number from memory.

"Hello, I'm trying to reach one of your guests, a Mr. George. Thanks." After a pause, "Hello, this is Clay Greer calling. I hope I'm not too late. My secretary left me a note asking me to call you today, even if it was late. I just drove in from southern Utah."

The party on the other end talked for a considerable time, while Clay sat down and listened patiently. Finally, there was a pause and Clay said, "Well, if you think it's really so important, I'll come right over for a few minutes. My office is just across the street. You'll be in the coffee shop? How will I recognize you? Okay." Clay hung up, stared into space for a moment, and left the office with lights blazing.

He walked the short distance from his office on Exchange Place to the hotel on the corner of Main Street and Fourth South and entered the Newhouse Hotel Coffee Shop, which was mostly deserted at this late hour. He spotted a large man in his late 60s with a curly shock of silver hair seated in an up-front booth. The man looked at him expectantly, and Clay introduced himself.

"Pleased to meet you, Mr. Greer," Mr. George said in a deep resonant voice with a faint accent, "I'm Blaine Issac George, mining investments. I'm up from Los Angeles on business in Salt Lake. I come here fairly often. I'm glad you were able to meet with me. I've heard a lot about you. Would you like something to eat?" He waved to the lone waitress, who had already started to move toward them when Clay seated himself in the booth.

"Sure," Clay answered, turning to the waitress. "Clairesse, I haven't eaten since noon. Bring me a slice of your famous pecan pie and coffee. And put a scoop of vanilla ice cream on the side." Turning back to Mr. George, he noticed a knowing look cross his face as the waitress turned to go to the kitchen.

"You're not a Mormon, I see," he remarked. "You're having coffee."

"Does that matter?" Clay asked.

"No, but I didn't know," Mr. George answered, "And I like to know the people I deal with."

They chatted to get acquainted with each other, and swapped names of mutual acquaintances in the mining business, as people in the mining game always did. It seemed Blaine George mostly knew mining promoters and stockbrokers from all over the West, and hardly knew any of the geologists and mining engineers who made up Clay's circle of friends and competitors. Clay thought to himself, Jeanie has a good point. If this guy has any money, he sure would make a good client.

"What was so urgent that we had to meet this evening?" Clay asked as he polished off the pie and a second cup of coffee. He knew from their conversation that Blaine George would be in Salt Lake for the rest of the week, so something else must be involved.

"Mr. Greer, I like what I have heard about you," he said, "and I believe I can trust you to hold my information in strict confidence. I was told that you are very professional, and would maintain a confidence. Can we go up to my room? I have something to show you."

Clay felt revived with something in his stomach, and said, "Sure, but make it brief. I have to go home and unpack a lot of dirty gear. I've been in the field for nearly a week."

"Oh, I'm dreadfully sorry. I know you must be anxious to see your wife. Do you have children?" George blustered, obviously embarrassed.

"No, I'm not married. But, as a bachelor I've got to do my own housekeeping. It's easy to get behind when you travel as much as I do."

In his hotel room, George opened a valise and pulled out a large buckskin pouch and laid it on the bed. Looking seriously at Clay, he said, "What I am going to disclose must remain secret from anyone else. Can I have your solemn pledge?" Clay nodded, holding up his right hand.

George reached into the pouch and took out a massive silver necklace, holding it and then placing it on the bed. He took out two other silver necklaces, placing them on the bed beside the first. Then he rummaged around in the pouch and scooped out several fragments of heavy silver jewelry and arranged them on the bed next to the necklaces. It made a strange array for a Mining Man to show to a consulting geologist, Clay thought.

"My hobby is collecting old Navajo jewelry and rugs, for investment purposes and because I enjoy them," he said. "I've followed my hobby for nearly 30 years, ever since I came to this country, and these are the most unusual pieces I have ever seen. Look at the stones mounted in these pieces, have you ever seen anything like them? I purchased them recently from an indian trader, as unredeemed pawn. He sold them to me cheap because neither of us knew what the unusual stones were. He thinks, and I agree, that these pieces are quite old." George sat down on the bed and watched Clay's face intently as he bent down to inspect the pieces.

The massive silver jewelry looked like authentic Navajo items sure enough, but primitive. They seemed to be quite old. The essentially colorless stone pebbles mounted in all of the pieces, even in the fragments of necklaces, looked like clear quartz, but had a greasy luster and a refractive brilliance that told him it wasn't common quartz. The rounded pebbles were water worn, and mounted as they had been originally found, without any cutting or polishing. Navajo jewelry almost always featured polished turquoise, which is a brilliant azure blue, or sometimes polished red coral. These colorless stones were positively plain in appearance, except for that hint of brilliance. No wonder the indian trader was happy to unload these odd pieces.

Clay held the largest mounted stone, probably an ounce or more in weight, up to the incandescent light bulb in the table lamp. Even in its rough unpolished form, the pebble looked different and seemed to refract light in a faint rainbow sheen. As Clay pondered, George came over, reached into the pile of jewelry fragments and extracted one piece containing a pebble that had been chipped. He picked up a glass ashtray and scratched the smooth bottom with the chipped pebble. It effortlessly left a deep groove.

"Wow," Clay responded, "Whatever it is, that stone sure is hard. It cut that glass like butter!" Inspecting the pebble in his hand more closely, he suspected it might be some colorless gemstone, because extreme hardness is an important feature in gemstones. He noted the clarity and clearness of the pebble, and remarked to himself that, whenever it was, it seemed to qualify as gem quality.

Clay reached into the open neck of his khaki shirt and pulled out a tiny magnifying lens attached to a leather thong around his neck. He placed it up to his right eye and looked intently at the pebble. He picked up another and peered at it also, turning the specimen slowly for a better view. He was looking for fractures and inclusions in the clear stones. Suddenly, he saw what he had been looking for—a tiny cluster of black specks. These were carbon inclusions, sure as hell, he thought to himself. Carbon inclusions are characteristic of the diamond, which is itself pure crystallized carbon. Carbon inclusions are also found in quartz, but this stone was much harder than quartz. On the other hand, carbon inclusions are seldom seen in other hard and colorless gemstones, like topaz, or the pale beryls and sapphires. Also, diamonds are the hardest of all gemstones. Clay felt confident as he said, "Mr. George, I can't tell for certain without further testing, but I think these might be diamonds."

Blaine Issac George burst into a broad smile. "I have searched long and hard for someone who could help me find the source of these diamonds. I knew you were the right man the moment we met," he blurted, adding, "Can you help me find the source of these remarkable stones?"

"Wait a minute," Clay replied. "How do you know that the stones didn't come from Africa, or anywhere, for that matter? The Navajos learned silversmithing from the early Mexicans, and how do we know some old Navajo didn't acquire some uncut diamonds and make them into a few pieces of jewelry? Anyhow, diamonds don't occur anywhere in the western United States, and certainly not in the Colorado Plateau. This could be a great waste of time, and lead us nowhere!"

"But everything points to a local source. Navajos, particularly early in this century, didn't have access to uncut diamonds, especially large gem quality alluvial stones. There is probably a deposit of diamonds out there somewhere, awaiting re-discovery by us! Think of it, we can both be rich!"

Clay stared at him with glazed eyes.

Calming himself, George continued, "I have researched this matter, and I think the stones come from a deposit somewhere in the northern part of the Navajo Reservation, possibly the San Juan River. I think early Navajos found these diamonds, mined them, and the stones wound up in pieces of jewelry. Possibly they never recognized their great value. Will you help me?"

Clay was somewhat overwhelmed and felt very tired from his long day. He realized he needed to get some sleep, and to think calmly about the remarkable events of this amazing evening.

"Look, Mr. George," he said, "I'm too tired to think rationally about this situation. I'll call you after I've had a chance to think further on this."

Blaine Issac George was disappointed in Clay's reaction, but clearly Clayton P. Greer was not a man to be rushed into any decision. In a calm but emphatic voice, he said, "Mr. Greer, I need your help. I need a man of your knowledge and broad field experience. Take some time and give it whatever thought you need, but I would like your decision before I return to Los Angeles at the end of the week. You can reach me at the hotel. I and my investor group are prepared to compensate you for your professional services and any expenses you incur investigating this matter on our behalf. Think about my proposal, then call me."

They shook hands and Clay headed back to his office. His energy reserves were now completely spent, and he decided to sleep the night on a folding canvas cot he kept in the storeroom for such occasions. All he had to do was retrieve his sleeping bag from the Jeep, shake out the dust and pull off his boots. He was asleep within minutes.

Back at the Newhouse Hotel, Mr. George placed his valuable jewelry pieces back in the buckskin pouch and sat on the edge of his bed, deep in thought.

The gusting south wind was rattling the windows. George looked at his watch, hesitated a moment, then picked up the telephone beside his bed. "Operator, I need to make a long distance call to Los Angeles." He gave a telephone number, then waited patiently. After a few moments a voice answered. "Hello, Paul, this is Blaine. I hope it isn't too late. Can you talk?" After a short response at the other end, George continued, "I met with the Salt Lake geologist we were told about, and I think he's the right man to do the job. I'm waiting to hear back from him. He seems quite cautious." There was more talk at the other end, and George replied, "He seems to think we are all crazy."

After a short exchange, George concluded the conversation, "Of course I will. In the meantime, will you call the others and inform them that I was successful in contacting him? I'll call you as soon as I know anything definite. Keep your fingers crossed." He hung up and stared at the closed door leading to the hallway, thinking of all the points he should have made in his discussion with Mr. Clayton P. Greer, but didn't.

He then slowly got up and started to undress his ample body. He debated whether to crack the window, but a sharp gust of wind convinced him otherwise. Down to his skivvies, he switched off the light and climbed into the bed. In a few minutes he was fast asleep, snoring heavily.

Unloading the 1954 Willys Jeep station wagon.

2

SCOPING THE PROJECT

Clay awoke at 7:30 the next morning, stiff from sleeping on the narrow cot. He felt refreshed, but grimy. He slowly wandered down the corridor to the small men's room. He dowsed his face with water in the wash basin, looking forward to a shower at home.

Back in his small office he pondered the events of last night. The prospect of looking for lost diamond deposits intrigued him, particularly with a client willing to pay the tab. Business was slow at this time of the year, and the proposal looked much better in the light of a new day. However, he needed someone to bounce ideas off as he devised some plan to present to Mr. George.

He reached for the telephone and dialed a number from memory. "Hello, Mary? Is Jerry around?" After a pause, "Hi, Jerry, its Clay. I've got a proposition I'd like to discuss with you. Have you got time later this morning?" After another short pause, "Sure, I can meet you at Lamb's for lunch, and I'll buy. That will give me some time to do some errands, anyhow." He hung up and thought for a moment, then dialed another number.

"Let me speak to Mr. George, please." he said, then, "Mr. George, this is Clay Greer. I've been thinking about our conversation. I want to explore some ideas with a business associate, a geologist friend who might be my field partner. Is it okay to discuss your information with him, in strict confidence, of course?" There was an excited exchange at the other end of the line, but after a short interval Clay said, "Look, I can't do this project alone, and this guy can be trusted. I'll vouch for him." There was another exchange, this time less excited, and finally Clay responded, "Sure, I can do that. I'm in my office right across the street. I think that's an excellent idea, and I'll meet you in the coffee shop in a half hour."

Clay fished out some clean khakis from his suitcase, went back to the men's room, and tried to comb his wild hair to look respectable. As he exited his office building he discovered that about four inches of wet snow had fallen, turning the gutters into slushy moats and causing sidewalk pedestrians to scatter whenever street traffic drove past. He was glad he was wearing field boots. Considering all the water-spattered people he encountered crossing the street to the Newhouse Hotel, his khakis and field jacket didn't look so bad.

As he entered the coffee shop Blaine George was sitting in the same upfront booth, and he slid in opposite him as he had done the night before. They exchanged greetings, and both ordered. George ordered coffee, dark toast and a half grapefruit. Clay ordered a ham omelet, coffee, rye toast and a large orange juice. They talked as they ate.

"Who is this individual you intend to use as a field assistant?" George asked. "You said he's a geologist. Do we need two geologists? How much do you think you need to tell him about our project?" George looked intently at Clay's face as he talked, trying to gauge Clay's reaction to his words.

Clay explained that Jerry Brooks, who held a degree in geology and had been a co-worker with Clay at his first job with a government agency, was currently the owner of a local rock shop, Jerry's Lapidary and Supplies. He described Jerry as about 45, ten years older than himself, and highly experienced in prospecting, particularly for something exotic like gemstones. He argued that he would need a second person in the field, as an assistant and for safety purposes, and that Jerry would bring a lot of useful expertise to the project. As Clay put it, for a single sub-professional wage he would be getting multiple needed talents in his friend, Jerry Brooks. A look of relief crossed George's face as Clay talked. He sensed that Clay was rising to the challenge, and he didn't want to do anything that would cause him to waiver. He agreed to let Clay discuss basic details of the project with Jerry Brooks, provided he first took a pledge of strict secrecy.

"Wait a minute," Clay responded. " I need to devise some feasible plan with Jerry's input before I'm willing to commit. His pledge of confidentially, the same as mine, is all you can get at this time. I'll vouch for his integrity, but that's it."

Blaine Issac George considered for a moment, then said, "You're right. If you are willing to vouch for him, I will accept that. But you need to get his solemn promise that he won't do anything to compete with us, or compromise our search for the diamonds." His voice lowered as he uttered the last words, and he looked around to see if anyone was listening.

Clay agreed, and George placed a small paper sack on the table in front of him. "Here are the fragments you looked at last night, with some of the less valuable stones to test as you see fit, and to show to Mr. Brooks if you decide to do so. Please return them to me." Clay agreed.

Mr. George picked up the breakfast tab, and Clay headed home. Later, dressed in a plaid shirt and corduroy trousers, with a hip length stylish wool car coat for warmth, Clay felt less like a field geologist as he drove downtown to meet Jerry Brooks at Lamb's Restaurant on Main Street.

Upon reflection, Lamb's as a place to meet wasn't very smart. Lamb's was an institution with the mining fraternity, if you could call it that. The clientele was almost exclusively downtown businessmen, which in Salt Lake City consisted of lawyers, mining company executives, stock promoters and stock brokers, all with strong connections to uranium speculation and the mining industry. Lamb's was a place to go and be seen, not a place to discuss secret matters. Clay's heart fluttered as he entered and was greeted by George Lamb himself.

"Mr. Greer, so nice to see you again. Your friend told me you would be coming and I've already seated him. Follow me," he said.

It seemed that every head in the place turned as Clay made his way back to Jerry's booth. Some customers greeted Clay by name, while others merely nodded in recognition. Man, this was definitely not a good place for a cozy noon luncheon on a business day, Clay thought to himself. Even Bob Bernick, the *Tribune* business editor was there, and looked up from his conversation with two prosperous looking men as Clay passed by. Clay felt like a five point buck on opening day of the deer hunting season.

"Good to see you, Clay," Jerry Brooks said. "What's this proposition you want to talk about?" Clay winced, and motioned Jerry to be less obvious. Clay responded a bit loudly, "Well, Jerry, you won our bet, so I am here to buy your lunch." He glanced around to see if anyone was listening.

Relieved, Clay leaned toward Jerry and said in a whisper, "Let's wait 'til later to discuss details. Just say I've got us an interesting project for the next month or so, if you can get away from the shop. Are you interested?" Jerry looked surprised, but nodded. They ordered from the menu presented to them by the matronly waitress in the restaurant's uniform, a white apron over a starched white dress, and white shoes.

Over lunch they discussed how slow their respective businesses were in the early part of 1957, the late winter season being extremely quiet at the rock shop, and certainly not a good season for Clay's field work, except in southern Arizona and Mexico. As they finished their meal, Clay said, "I'm parked on the street outside, and I don't want to pay more to a parking meter, so why don't we get together at your shop? Parking there is no problem." Jerry agreed, and they made their way to the cash register at the entrance of the crowded restaurant, nodding to acquaintances and stopping briefly to exchange pleasantries. Clay was limp with relief as they reached the sidewalk. His relief was premature.

John S. Arcarius, a slick promoter of dubious mining opportunities and a notorious deal hijacker, was just about to enter the restaurant.

"Well, Clay, glad to see you're back in town!" he said with too much enthusiasm. "Too bad the ore samples you tested didn't turn out as good as anticipated. Those Texas fellows backed away from my venture after they read your report and saw the assay results. You should have come back for a further look." The look on his face was suddenly menacing. "Maybe someday I will be able to repay the favor!" He looked closely at Jerry, but dismissed him as someone unimportant and passed on inside. Holy Mother, Clay thought, I sure hope he doesn't get wind of this new project!

Back at Jerry's store-front rock shop on the outskirts of Salt Lake's run down west side, Jerry and Clay settled into a cluttered back room with a large work table and shelves of inventory lining the walls. There was a large map of Utah pinned to an open space on one side. They sat in folding chairs next to the table. Clay opened the conversation.

"Jerry, you won't believe what I'm going to tell you, but first I want to solemnly swear you to secrecy. Do you agree?" Jerry nodded and Clay continued, "I met last night with this guy from Los Angeles, his name is Blaine Issac George, and he showed me some large alluvial diamonds he thinks came from somewhere near the Navajo Indian Reservation, on the Utah side. He wants to hire me to see if I can figure out exactly where. I told him I would need a field assistant, and I recommended you. You interested?"

Jerry sat for a moment in dumbfounded silence. Then he chuckled and said, "Holy Moley, Clay, this guy is crazy, and so are you if you believe him! Diamonds don't occur anywhere in the West, and certainly not anywhere near the Navajo reservation. Are you pulling my leg?"

Clay assured him that the guy seemed legitimate, and then showed him the jewelry fragments. Jerry examined them closely with a hand lens, then a binocular microscope, and finally with a Mohs hardness testing kit. He concurred that the stones tested exceptionally hard and looked like diamonds, and from that point on he became more serious. They talked about how diamonds might have come into the possession of an early Navajo silversmith, and how it might be possible for a deposit to exist somewhere and yet not be known to anyone except Navajos. The more they talked, the more excited they both became, and a plan began to emerge.

Clay went over to the wall map, and pointed. "Here, near the northern boundary of the Navajo indian reservation, is where George purchased the jewelry, and where he thinks we ought to look, but I'm not so sure…"

"What is your opinion? Somewhere in the San Juan Mountains?" Jerry asked.

"Before we get too carried away with this whole proposition, I want someone more knowledgeable than the two of us to certify that these really are diamonds," Clay said.

Jerry thought for a minute, then got up to find the telephone book. "I used to know a jeweler who specialized in colored gemstones, a guy I would consult when someone tried to sell me rough or cut gem materials. He had lots of fancy equipment and seemed to know how to use it. He saved my hide more than once, identifying stones represented as being one kind of gemstone, when it actually was something else. He also educated me on how easy, and common, it is to treat common gemstones to enhance their color, or minimize flaws. He really knew his stuff." After turning a few pages in the classified yellow pages, he said, "Here's the guy, Waterford Jewelry on Twenty-First South in Sugarhouse. Eph Waterford. You want me to call him?"

Jerry dialed the number and arranged for a test. Clay pried a stone out of the jewelry fragment, and Jerry represented it as something he had acquired in a trade with another mineral dealer, which had been represented to him as being an alluvial diamond. Waterford was asked to confirm its identity, and to estimate its value as a rough stone.

In the cluttered back room of his shop Eph Waterford carefully inspected the stone, measured its index of refraction on the refractometer, performed sev-

21

eral hardness tests, and even burned a small chip of the specimen that had come off during a hardness test. Both Clay and Jerry were surprised that the chip would burn so easily, forming a clear gas without any residue whatsoever. Waterford pointed out that, since diamond is a crystalized form of carbon, the diamond combines readily with oxygen under intense heat, to form carbon dioxide. "Everyone is taught that a diamond is hard and indestructible," he said, "so it comes as a big surprise to see it disappear when heated in air. But burning small fragments of suspected diamonds is a time honored test for the real thing. No other hard gemstone reacts the same way." Clay took mental notes.

Waterford turned out to be quite an expert, although diamonds were not his favorite gemstone. "Too much advertising, and not enough real value," he remarked to them more than once. His favorite was the emerald, which he explained was much more costly, weight for weight, than the diamond and all other gemstones. Asked about the value of their sample, Waterford remarked that it looked very clear and was apparently flawless. He estimated that possibly up to ten carats of cut and faceted diamonds of various sizes and shapes could be produced from this single pebble. He guessed that the wholesale value of this stone might be $5,000, possibly more. Clay gasped, knowing that Blaine George had many larger stones in his buckskin pouch.

Their business concluded, Jerry asked Waterford to bill him, and they left. By now it was late afternoon, and Clay was faced with the prospect of driving Jerry back to the rock shop so he could ride home with Mary, who had Jerry's pickup truck. As they contemplated the long drive on the crowded cross-town streets at rush hour, Jerry suggested instead that they go directly to his home near Sugarhouse. He could telephone Mary to come directly home. Jerry and Clay could use the time for more planning and Clay could stay for supper. Mary and her daughters were excellent cooks.

Arriving at Jerry's, Clay parked the Jeep at the curb of the quiet street. Inside, Jerry's daughters were home from school, and someone had whipped up a batch of cookies. He and Jerry scooped up a plate full from the kitchen, grabbed some cold beers from the refrigerator, and headed to Jerry's small office in the basement. Jerry had a large map of Utah stapled to one wall, identical to the one at the rock shop. It would be invaluable for their planning, which was now in dead earnest.

First, they had to come up with a plan, and a timetable, for testing their hypothesis that diamonds could be found in river gravels. There were many questions. Which river? How does one prospect river gravels to find diamonds? What equipment is needed? How much time will it take to prove their hypothesis, one way or the other? How can they estimate travel and subsistence expenses for the test period? Where should they start; where should they go next? Will other personnel be needed, and if so, how many, and whom?

Later that evening, after dinner, they completed their plan and a budget of sorts. Clay telephoned Blaine George to arrange a meeting the next morning. Next he telephoned his secretary at her apartment, to come into the office early Tuesday morning to type up the proposal. Then Clay went home and slept in his own bed for the first time in over a week, but he hardly slept at all. Several times he sat up in bed, wide awake, turned on a bedside lamp and jotted notes in the margins of the pages of notes that he and Jerry had compiled.

About 7:30 the next morning Clay was in his office, impatiently waiting for Jeanie to arrive. She opened the front door at precisely 8:00 and sat down to type the several pages of notes into a comprehensible report, as only Jeanie could do. He busied himself cutting and coloring maps and diagrams as illustrations. Shortly before 9:00 Jerry showed up, and they rehearsed their presentation. As soon as everything was ready, Clay called Mr. George and they headed for the Newhouse Hotel.

At precisely ten o'clock Clay introduced Gerald Brooks and they launched into their proposal. It would involve up to three months of fieldwork for both. Clay's professional fee would be $150 per day and Jerry would work for $80 per day. Meals, mileage and supplies were estimated for the entire project. It came to a grand total of $23,000. As Clay pointed out, about five moderately sized diamonds would cover the entire outlay, and the client could shut down the whole project at any time on ten days notice. As a success bonus, Clay and Jerry wanted a 20% share of the diamonds produced from any deposit they might discover, less their share of operating (mining) expenses, with operating costs to be carried by Mr. George and his investors until Clay and Jerry received sufficient cash flow to cover their own share of the mine operating costs.

Blaine George had listened quietly, and he inspected the typed report closely. "You have done a thorough job, Mr. Greer, as I was led to expect from you. The financial charges in the proposal are acceptable, and I will leave the operational details entirely up to you. You have my complete confidence. As for Mr. Brooks, he should make a very capable field assistant. Finally, with respect to the bonus you so rightly request, I think it is a bit too much. I know my investor partners, and I think they would insist upon a limit of no more than 15%, to commence only after they have recovered 200% of their capital and operating expense outlays, that is, until payout. Would that be acceptable?"

Clay looked at Jerry, and they turned to George. "When can we start?"

Blaine Issac George got up from the chair, all smiles, both hands extended. "I'll write you a check for $1,000 and you can start as soon as you are able. Well, gentlemen, I've got some telephone calls to make. Will you excuse me?"

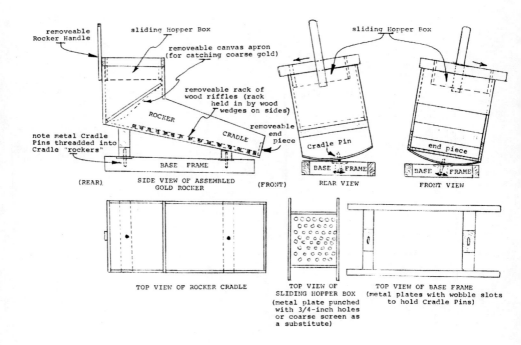

Plans for a portable gold rocker.

3

THE DRIVE SOUTH

During the remainder of the week, Clay spent most of his time at the U.S. Geological Survey library in Salt Lake City reading everything he could find about prospecting for diamonds. He also read all he could find about the mineral resources of southeastern Utah, but he didn't find any mention of ultramafic rocks, the host rock where diamonds are formed. He also purchased a set of topographic maps covering the area that he and Jerry had targeted.

He learned that high altitude aerial photography had been flown recently by the USGS along part of the San Juan River, so he ordered complete stereoscopic coverage from the available photos within the area of interest. Clay loved working with aerial photos, particularly where there was stereoscopic coverage. Bent over a stereoscope looking at the miniature three-dimensional landscape in the photos, he felt like he was suspended in air over the landforms below. It was an awesome feeling, especially over the rugged topography of southeastern Utah's canyon country. To a geologist, it was as good as actually being there.

After several days of library research, Clay felt it was time to report to Blaine George, and make some final plans for their fieldwork. They again met at the Newhouse Hotel coffee shop. Clay filled him in on his research and progress.

"Do either you or Mr. Brooks speak Navajo?" Mr. George asked. Clay shook his head. George continued, "I do, but not very much. You will need to find someone trustworthy to translate for you. Few reservation Navajos speak English, or Spanish, only their native language. Do you know the story of the Navajo Code Talkers of World War II?" Clay said he didn't.

"In the South Pacific the U.S. Marines had trouble with the Japanese soldiers listening in on their radio transmissions," George explained. "Many Japanese could understand the English language so everything the Marines communicated was heard by the Japanese. Some convenient code language was desperately needed. There were numerous Navajos in the Marine units, and most of them were fluent in the Navajo language. Somebody had the idea to use Navajos as radio operators, talking in the Navajo language to other Navajo radio operators. They were recruited from all units, and it worked. Of course, the Japanese were completely baffled and never figured out the code the Marines were using. The Navajo Nation is very proud of those Code Talkers, as they were known throughout the Pacific Theater of War."

"Were you in the war?" Clay asked.

George stared at Clay for a long time, then replied, "If you mean World War I, then the answer is Yes. Actually, I was a young officer in the Cossacks, in the Army of the Russian Czar. Fortunately I never served on the European Front, and when the Revolution against the Czar erupted toward the end of World War I, I was able to escape across Siberia and ultimately I emigrated to the United States."

"You were in the Army of the Russian Czar?" Clay exclaimed.

"Yes," George replied, "Russia under the Czar was quite different from Russia today. The Bolshevik Revolution changed everything. I was lucky to get out alive. I rode across Siberia on the last train east out of the Ural Mountains, across frozen lakes on temporary rails and ties laid directly on the lake ice each winter. On one warm day the weight of the train caused the rotten ice to sink and the water to well up and overflow the tracks, so that it looked like the train was driving into the lake itself. I was very relieved when we reached the opposite shoreline."

George seemed to enjoy telling Clay about his past, and Clay was enthralled. When they parted, Clay had a much deeper respect for his client.

While Clay had been researching the literature, Jerry had been equally busy, researching equipment used in alluvial prospecting and mining. He had a skilled carpenter construct a portable gold rocker according to plans he had copied out of a book on gold placer prospecting, which he felt would apply directly to alluvial diamond prospecting. The portable gold rocker would prove to be a great labor saving device in the field. He ordered a set of portable screens from a catalog, and bought gold pans, portable ultraviolet lamps and some hand tools from his own rock shop inventory.

By the end of the week Clay was convinced he had learned everything he could from books, and he had cleared his desk of the unfinished work for his other clients. He was ready to head for the field.

Jerry made arrangements with his wife, Mary, to staff the rock shop during the remainder of the season until late April or early May, when he figured the project would be concluded. He also made arrangements with her to ship the portable gold rocker and the mail order screens to him by Trailways bus as soon as they arrived.

When the carpenter called to inform Jerry that the portable gold rocker would be delivered on Monday morning, Clay and Jerry scheduled their departure for later that day. They would drive down in Clay's 1954 Jeep station wagon since it had four-wheel drive and a power winch on the front bumper. It was the ideal vehicle for the rough backcountry. It would be a slow highway trip in the Jeep, but they planned several stops enroute. The boxy station wagon would be tightly packed with all the gear, but it was adequate.

Monday morning Clay headed over to Jerry's shop, where the carpenter was already unloading the gold rocker. As Clay walked up, Jerry said, "Clay, this sure worked out well. This little baby will save a lot of backbreaking labor when we go to sampling the gravel deposits." Jerry explained to Clay how the rocker separated the finer material from the course gravel, causing the fine material to pass over riffles which trap the heavier components (including any gold and diamonds) while allowing the lighter component to wash out the lower end. Water is poured over the raw gravel, and sloshed through the screen and riffles by a steady rocking motion. It takes two men to operate, but it processes more material than a gold pan and with a lot less labor. Its name rocker came from the rocking motion of the cradle during operation. It was a simple operation that both of them would get to know well in the coming weeks.

Since the rocker was too big to fit inside, they tied it onto the roof of the Jeep. Just then the Parcel Post truck drove up and delivered the screens. What luck, Jerry thought. Now Mary won't have to ship them.

Jerry quickly put his duffle and the screens, still in their packing, into the back of the Jeep. Clay paid the carpenter while Jerry kissed Mary goodbye, and they drove off toward the south, bound for southeast Utah at last.

Heading south along State Street, which was U.S. Highway 91 when it passed through the city, they crossed Point of the Mountain at 10:30 and soon left Salt Lake Valley behind them. Ahead lay smoky Utah Valley, dominated by lofty Mount Timpanogos looming to the east and muddy Utah Lake on the west. The Geneva Plant of U.S. Steel Corporation, a curious relic of World War II, and the old Ironton Iron Smelter, a Mormon pioneer relic, were the source of the smoke and haze that besmudged this pastoral valley. An arcing string of Mormon agricultural communities, centered on the town of Provo, filled the fertile strip of land between the mountain and the lake. U.S. Highway 91 ran through each community along the eastern and southern shores of Utah Lake, until it exited Utah Valley and headed southwesterly across empty sagebrush hills and arid deserts to Cedar City, Las Vegas and ultimately to Los Angeles.

About 45 miles south of Salt Lake City U.S. Highway 6 & 50 branches off toward the southeast, climbing up Spanish Fork Canyon toward the coal mining town of Price on the other side of the Wasatch Range. The highway then continues southeasterly across 60 miles of barren sage and jimsonweed flats to the isolated community of Green River, then easterly on to Grand Junction, Colorado, a bustling small city and the business center of the West Slope of the Colorado Rockies.

About 20 miles beyond Green River on the highway to Grand Junction, less traveled highway U.S. 160 branches due south about 20 miles to a tiny oasis community on the Colorado River curiously named Moab. The small Mormon community of Moab was the Utah center of the Colorado Plateau Uranium Boom, then at its height in 1957. Ultimately U.S. 160 continues further south to the even smaller community of Monticello, then turns east toward Cortez, Colorado. A paved state highway, Utah 47, runs from Monticello south to the small Mormon communities of Blanding and Bluff, and finally through an even smaller community called Mexican Hat, then across the San Juan River and onto the vast Navajo Indian Reservation. There it becomes a gravel road ultimately connecting with an Arizona highway coming up from the south. None of these insignificant places have any meaning except to their few inhabitants or the uranium prospectors swarming over the canyons and plateaus in the vicinity, and to the readers of this story. In between these isolated settlements there is nothing but emptiness, arid plateaus, wide sweeps of high desert, rock ledges, cliffs and deep canyons.

Clay drove these lonely stretches a lot, and when he drove alone, as he often did, he would sing or recite poetry to himself, or engage in exercises of the mind to keep himself awake. But with a passenger aboard, especially an old friend like Jerry, he could engage in stimulating conversations about subjects of mutual interest. It made the miles fly by, and it kept him awake.

"Jerry," he said as they left populous Utah Valley behind them and headed up Spanish Fork Canyon toward Soldier Summit on U.S. Highway 6 & 50, "Do you know how this canyon got its name?"

Jerry allowed as how he didn't, so Clay continued, "Back in the fur trapper days they knew that the region south of Utah Lake belonged to Spain and that the area to the north belonged to America, as part of the Oregon Territory. They decided that the actual boundary between the U.S. and Mexico was the Provo River, where it runs into Utah Lake. So they named the first canyon to the north American Fork, and the first canyon to the south Spanish Fork. They turned out to be a little off in their reckoning, but the names stuck."

"Gosh, Clay, how do you come to know things like that?" Jerry asked.

"Well, if you'd spent as many nights alone in motel rooms and mining camps as I have, you read a lot. I'm partial to books on western history and exploration. It adds a certain flavor to all this scenery," he replied.

Both Clay and Jerry were full of stories, so they kept up this banter as the long drive wore on. There was no reception on the Jeep's AM radio away from the large towns, except late at night when darkness and weather sometimes allowed reception of the stronger radio stations. KSL in Salt Lake City broadcast at a powerful 50,000 watts, or so they said. Many nights, camped out on some ridge or mountaintop, or driving late at night, Clay had relished listening to broadcasts from home, and to the wonderful orchestral music KSL beamed into the hinterland "and to ships at sea" as the announcer often said.

Coming down Price Canyon on the other side of the Wasatch Range, the highway led past coal mine portals in the canyon's cliffs and past the little railroad community of Helper, until they drove out onto a flat expanse east of the mountains and into the bustling community of Price. Price was a notorious settlement of mostly Greek coal miners and other non-Mormons, an island of gentiles in the sea of rural Mormons who thinly populated the rest of Utah. Price was a mecca for ethnic non-Mormons, with its whiskey bars, rumored gambling and bawdy houses, all winked at by the local law enforcement.

Clay gassed up in downtown Price, bought both of them a cold pop, and headed southeast into the desolate flats of the Green River Desert that stretched south between the lofty Book Cliffs on the east and the awesome steeply up-heaved formations of the San Rafael Swell, far to the southwest. The bleak hilly terrain over which the highway meandered was mostly blackish Mancos shale, which weathered to a battleship gray and wouldn't even support healthy sage-brush. The entire region between Price and Green River was exceptionally barren. Small selenite gypsum crystals in the clayey hillsides glistened in the bright March sun, causing Clay to squint and feel sleepy.

Clay glanced over at Jerry, and noticed he was beginning to nod off in the warm sunshine streaming in through the windshield. He decided to keep them both awake by telling another story. "Do you know the story of Vernon Pick and the uranium mine he discovered on the Muddy River, back in the heart of the San Rafael Swell country?" Jerry startled awake. "It's a story of blind luck or government favoritism, depending on which story you choose to believe."

Without waiting for Jerry to respond, Clay continued, "Vern was a midwesterner, some kind of a mechanic, who didn't know a lick about uranium prospecting when he showed up in Utah and found a rich uranium deposit in the most remote country you can ever imagine. How he came to be at that spot, and how he came to recognize the uranium deposit for what it was, is a mystery to local folks who knew him and the country. But he was sure lucky. It turned out to be a good mine, and he took out lots of rich ore. The U.S. Atomic Energy Commission publicity boys sure were proud of Vernon Pick, and his story was widely published in newspapers and magazines. It certainly encouraged a lot of folks to come to this desolate region to try their luck at uranium prospecting. Some folks think a couple of government geologists who were rim flying the rugged terrain in a small airplane and using really sophisticated equipment looking for uranium signs, put Vernon onto such a remote uranium deposit. The AEC had a small field camp at Temple Mountain, right in the center of the San Rafael Swell, and they had a team of seasoned geologists looking for uranium deposits similar to those already known to occur at Temple Mountain. You know, there are oil seeps all throughout the San Rafael Swell, and uranium has an affinity for hydrocarbons. Uranium, if it is dissolved in the ground water, will tend to accumulate on or in association with any organic materials and oily hydrocarbons. Organic accumulations can form a commercial uranium deposit under favorable conditions.

Well, anyhow, several of the folks from the AEC camp wound up working for Pick, after he got rich! It made some folks suspicious. What really keeps tongues wagging in the uranium patch is the way Pick sold the mine to a New York millionaire for nine or ten million in cash, just before the ore ran out. Talk about luck," Clay laughed. "Vernon Pick was my kinda guy, he made the millionaire kick in a war surplus Navy PBY seaplane, and then he took the money and moved to California."

Aware that Jerry would probably doze off as soon as he stopped talking, Clay asked, "Jerry, weren't you in the military during World War II?"

Jerry sat up, seemed to become more alert, and replied, "Yes, but I was nearly 30 years old when war was declared in 1941, so I enlisted in the Army Corps of Engineers. Because I had a college degree in geology, I wound up being assigned to the Office of Strategic Materials. I spent most of the war in Brazil, representing the OSM and encouraging maximum production of quartz crystals. Quartz crystals from Brazil are unique in the world and were used to the make radio oscillators, you know, the wafer shaped crystals that allow radios to transmit and receive on a discrete frequency. It was a very important part of the war effort since two-way radios were needed in ships, aircraft and for the battle troops. I lived in the Brazilian city of Belo Horizonte and found myself working with two Americans who had a network of suppliers of quartz crystals in that part of Brazil. One was aptly named Gyp Withers and the other was Bud Ingram. They certainly knew their business and had a good thing going, for sure. They made out well, selling critical quartz material to the U.S. government. They instructed their roving quartz buyers to purchase any gemstones and rare specimens they came across, and those two fellows really accumulated quite a collection of tourmalines, topazes and some of the most beautiful quartz crystal points you ever saw. Some of them were later sold to the Smithsonian Museum in Washington.

"Toward the end of the war I was relocated back to the U.S. and worked for the Manhattan Project, researching uranium resources to feed the atomic bomb project. I was in on the very beginnings of the Uranium Boom. After the end of the war I joined the U.S. Geological Survey and lived in Grand Junction, where you and I first met."

"Why did you leave the USGS," Clay inquired, "And how did you come to own your rock shop?"

"Well, while I was with the USGS I continued to work on uranium, in collaboration with what ultimately became the U.S. Atomic Energy Commission. We worked out of a log house in the back of a lumberyard in Grand Junction, near where the big AEC compound is today. Mary and I had married before I went into the Corps of Engineers, but during the war she lived with her family in Salt Lake. After I was assigned to Grand Junction, she and our small children joined me there. We had a small house, and were enjoying married life. Mary missed her family, her parents and siblings, but we could still travel back to Salt Lake at Christmas and for visits. We were quite happy. After a while the USGS decided to assign me to Washington, D.C. to work at a desk. I didn't want to move back east to the Washington area, so I turned down the assignment. You know what happens to your career when you refuse an assignment," he said, looking over at Clay.

"Anyhow," he continued, "We both wanted to return to Utah, but good geologists were out walking the streets in the early 1950s, looking for any kind of work. Jobs were scarce. Mary's uncle, Cleon Petersen, had a small rock shop in Salt Lake City and wanted to turn over the business to someone in the family. My love of gems and minerals, acquired when I worked in Brazil, prompted me to seriously consider buying him out. I had a government retirement account that I could take as a lump sum if I left government service, so I decided to quit the USGS job in Grand Junction, take my retirement money and buy the shop. It wasn't much of a business, but then we didn't have much money. I've never had any second thoughts or regrets. Over the years, I've expanded the shop's line of lapidary and prospecting equipment, and gotten into some exotic minerals you don't often find in rock shops. All the current interest in uranium prospecting has really been good for the equipment side of the business, especially in the summer season. The winter season, especially after Christmas, is slow, so this diamond hunting project comes along at a good time." Turning to face Clay, Jerry said, "Clay, I really want to thank you for considering me for a part in it. You really are a good friend."

"Hell, Jerry, you're the best. I ought to be thanking you." Clay responded, "Mary and your girls have been a big factor in your career decisions, haven't they?"

"Sure," Jerry replied, "She's a good Mormon girl and I'm a mighty poor Mormon boy, but we both love the West. Mary is determined that the girls get a good religious upbringing, and eventually marry into the Church." He smiled and turned to Clay, who smiled in return. Clay knew that The Church meant The Church of Jesus Christ of Latter Day Saints, known locally and elsewhere as the Mormons. "Everybody has got to be some place," Jerry said, "And I can't think of a better place than Salt Lake for us to be. But I don't think I'd like to live in one of those small Mormon rural communities," he said.

"Well, you need to be ready to shift gears for the next few weeks, 'cause we're going to be living right amongst 'em." Clay said, laughing.

"Maybe so, but Moab has gotten very cosmopolitan in the last couple of years with so many outlander prospectors, government men and mining promoters moving in to dilute the local Mormon population," Jerry replied. "Heck, Moab even has a state liquor store, which is more than you can say for Blanding. There's even an Elks Club in Moab, with an open bar for its members. Clay, did you know I'm a card carrying member of the Elks?"

"I'm mighty glad to hear it. We might need a good stiff drink before this project is finished. I knew I'd hired a real talent when I choose you, but I'm learning that you have many unsuspected extra qualities," Clay said, then added, "Seriously, Jerry, I didn't know how far you went back in the uranium business. Do you know a guy in Moab named Howard Balling who operates, or once operated, a gold placer mine on the Colorado River? He is known as Mr. Uranium because he dates from the old days of Madame Curie and the World War I era of radium mines in the Moab area and western Colorado. I was told to look him up, since he's the only living expert on mining alluvial deposits in this entire area."

"You bet, I knew Howard Balling from when I worked for the USGS," Jerry replied, "He's an elderly man, a real gentleman, and highly experienced in every phase of prospecting and mining. It doesn't surprise me to hear that he has operated a placer gold mine on the Colorado River, or that he is an acknowledged expert on the subject. If he's still in the area, he shouldn't be hard to find. I'll be happy to introduce you. I'd like to get reacquainted with him again. He could really tell some stories about early mining for radium, vanadium and uranium."

Jerry stared out the vehicle window in silence for a few minutes, then continued, "You know, the Uravan area along the Utah-Colorado border has a long and interesting history. Carnotite, the bright yellow uranium-vanadium oxide mineral everyone is prospecting for today, was used by the Ute Indians for face paint and to color objects. Europeans started using carnotite from Russia to color glazed pottery and china plates. The early underground gold miners of southwestern Colorado, near Ouray, ran into a black ooze they called pitchblende, actually a uranium oxide not so complex as carnotite. Pitchblende wasn't valuable for anything then, although it's the most valuable uranium ore today. Anyhow, some enterprising sole started shipping Colorado carnotite to Europe for use in pottery glazing, and it got to be quite well known. Madame Curie, a French scientist, isolated radium from carnotite and around World War I she personally came to western Colorado to supervise mining carnotite ores for the commercial extraction of radium, used for luminescent clock and watch dials, and for medical purposes.

"She set up an extraction plant outside Denver, at what is now called Rocky Flats. When radioactive radium was found to cause severe health problems, and death, radium mining and utilization dropped off. Then somebody found that vanadium, which occurs with uranium in carnotite ores, could be alloyed with steel to make armor plate and other extremely hard kinds of steel. Vanadium mining took off in the 1920s and 1930s, but the uranium by-product was worthless, and was discarded in the mill tailings. When the atom bomb project of World War II launched the search for uranium supplies, we looked into reprocessing the old vanadium mill tailings to recover the uranium. It worked, but the existing mill tailings weren't enough to fill the government's needs, so the government launched a vigorous campaign to discover more uranium resources, and set up a government monopoly to buy all domestic uranium ores."

After another pause, Jerry continued, "You know, it's illegal to sell uranium ores and concentrates to anyone except the federal government, but the AEC has a guaranteed ore buying program for all uranium ores produced, plus bonuses for opening a new mine and for producing high grade ores. It really has turned out to be a good deal, a government guaranteed good deal, for the uranium miners and prospectors. That explains why so many ordinary folks are attracted to uranium prospecting."

Clay already knew some of what Jerry had said, but he was impressed that Jerry knew so much and could spiel out so much information so succinctly.

"You know, it could all come crashing down if the government buying program is ended, as all things must eventually end," Jerry said, and fell silent.

Ahead, the isolated community of Green River, with its lush green cottonwood groves along the banks of the Green River came into sight. An oasis in an immense desert, and a beckoning stopping place for the traveler, Clay thought. "It's getting late, and it'll be dark in about an hour. I say we stop here for the night, 'cause I need to look up a bush pilot we'll need later on. Is that okay with you?" Clay said.

"You bet," replied Jerry. "Do we have time to untie the gold rocker and try it out on the gravel deposits down by the river? I've never actually used a gold rocker and I want to be sure it works okay."

"Well, of course. Let's find a secluded spot to try it out. I don't want anyone to get curious about what we're up to," Clay said. "I can look up my pilot friend after dark."

They drove through the center of the small business district, down to the highway bridge across the river. Clay parked the Jeep at one abutment and they both got out, stretching their cramped muscles. Clay walked out onto the bridge, looking up and down the river to find a likely gravel bar. He spotted a patch upstream near the river's edge with a dirt track leading to it. "Perfect," he muttered.

In minutes they were at the river's edge and had untied the rocker. Clay dragged it further upstream, until it was shielded from view by trees and tall brush. "Here, Jerry, show me how this contraption works," Clay called out. Jerry came up with a shovel and a big can fastened to the end of a short wooden pole.

"Shovel some gravel into the hopper, there, and I'll operate the rocker. You operate the dipper," Jerry said, pointing. Clay looked around, scooped up two or three shovels of marble sized gravel and dumped them into the hopper. Then he dipped the can on the pole into the river and filled it with water.

"Slowly pour the water into the hopper, as I rock the cradle," Jerry said as he started to shake the cradle. Jerry said, "Go fill the can again, pour it into the hopper, and keep on doing that until I tell you to stop." After about four cans of water the sandy material in the gravel had washed out of the rocker, leaving the coarser pebbles on the screen, and a lot of sandy material trapped behind the wooden riffles. "Ain't that neat?" Jerry said, looking up at Clay.

"I see," Clay said. "The heavy portion of the sandy material is caught in the riffles, while the light portion is washed overboard. Pretty slick, and it works just like you said. What happens if we dig out a diamond, one that won't pass through the screen?"

"Well," Jerry replied, "If something as big as a marble can't be identified as a diamond, we're in deep trouble." They both laughed, and switched places to process another load. After they had run five hopper loads of gravel through, which took about 15 minutes, they stopped and removed the heavy material trapped behind the riffles. They removed the transverse wooden riffles, unlatching the removable end of the cradle, and flushing the material in the bottom of the cradle into a waiting gold pan. After Jerry had placed the rocker concentrate in one of his gold pans, he stooped at the water's edge and began to pan the material.

"Hah, I knew it!" Clay snorted in mock surprise, "In the end you still have to do stoop labor." After panning for a few minutes, Jerry stood up and squinted into the tiny blackish sands in the bottom of the pan. Even in the fading light, he could see a single fleck of gold. He passed it to Clay. Just then they spotted two scruffy looking men standing in the trees. Clay and Jerry stared at the men for a full minute, then without a word, started disassembling the rocker and gathering up their equipment. By the time they had reloaded the Jeep and tied the rocker back on top, the men were gone.

"Who did they look like to you?" Clay said to Jerry, who just shrugged and shook his head.

Willys Jeep station wagon on the highway.

4

MOAB

Clay checked them into the Green Well Motel, where they would share a single room with two beds. As they looked over their sparse quarters, Jerry said, "I wonder if that radio in the night stand works? You know, recently I stayed at a hotel in Denver that had a television set. I don't suppose that Green River even has television reception."

"I doubt if Green River even has radio reception," Clay responded. He reached down and turned on the radio and got only a low buzz of static. "Oh well, maybe reception will improve later in the evening."

Clay pulled out a small notebook, turned several pages, and picked up the telephone on the nightstand. He dialed a number. "Is Jim Hewitt in? Thanks, I'll wait." After a few moments, "Hi, Jim, this is Clay Greer. You remember me, from last fall? Well, I'm going to need a good bush pilot in a couple of weeks. You available?" After a pause, "Great, can we drop by after dinner? Your office is still in the hanger where you keep your airplanes, isn't it?" Clay listened intently, then said goodbye and hung up. "Let's eat," he said.

They drove a short distance down the highway, turned into a short side street and parked in front of the Wayside Cafe. As they entered the dungeon-like interior, all eyes turned in their direction as they took seats in a rough hewn side booth. A woman behind the long counter leaned over and said in a loud voice, "You boys want a menu?" Clay and Jerry nodded, and stared back at the small crowd.

"What's that strange looking contraption on top of your Jeep?" a deep voice asked from the back of the room.

Clay focused on three scroungey looking men sitting behind beer mugs. Two of them must be the men we saw down by the river, he thought. "Don't try to answer them," Clay said in a low voice to Jerry.

They ordered from the menu and talked quietly as they ate. As they were finishing, the three in the back of the room got up and walked toward the cash register at the front of the cafe. As they passed Clay got his first good look.

When the three men had left, Clay turned to Jerry. "I recognize two of those guys, Lonnie and Willie Baker, brothers who call themselves prospectors but who are famous for claim jumping. They're bad news." Clay got up and walked quickly to the front door. Just as he suspected, the three men where inspecting the rocker, and one was peering into the Jeep. Clay stepped outside. "Please don't touch the vehicle," he said in a loud voice. The three men looked back, startled, and shuffled off to a dilapidated pickup truck. Clay stared after them as they got in and drove slowly away.

When they were out of sight, Clay returned to the booth. "Those guys are curious as hell, and up to no good."

After dinner Clay and Jerry drove the short distance to a large barnlike structure surrounded by light aircraft, which turned out to be the ramp of the Green River airport, a single gravel runway practically in the heart of the low buildings that made up the commercial center of town. It was the convenient home base of Green River Flying Service, a one-man operation run by Jim Hewitt.

A brightly lighted window at one corner of the hanger identified Hewitt's office, and they stepped inside. A rangy young man in his thirties looked up from a cluttered desk. "Hello, Clay. Good to see you again."

"Jerry, meet the best bush pilot in the Colorado Plateau and all of Canyon Country. Jim, here, introduced a new standard when it comes to flying off short dirt strips at high altitude. He's the guy who invented the prominent bump at the end of short landing strips, to bounce the airplane into the air when you run out of runway. It's scary, but it works."

Clay then explained to Jim their prospecting plans and that they wanted him to fly them around the Blanding area and meet them somewhere on the San Juan River. Clay didn't exactly know the place, or the time, when he needed Jim to come back, so they decided to telephone Jim from Blanding when they knew more. They negotiated a charter fee and Jim pencilled in some approximate dates on his scheduling calendar. They spent the rest of the evening swapping hanger talk. Clay was also a private pilot, but he clearly stood in awe of the abilities and experiences of Jim Hewitt, the bush pilot of the Green River Desert.

Jerry listened in amazement as Jim and Clay told tales of Jim's desert and canyon flying exploits that defied belief, of flying off the abrupt edge of vertical cliffs and swooping down canyons to gain flying speed, of hauling overloaded aircraft into the sky out of rough bulldozed landing strips back in areas so remote that it would take several days to jeep in, even when the weather permitted ground travel. Jim's air taxi service was much in demand by well financed prospecting teams and government geologists, most of whom didn't comprehend the limitations of light aircraft operations.

Clay impressed on Jerry the wonder of viewing the labyrinth of deep canyons from above, soaring from cliff face to opposite cliff face in less than a minute, whereas it could take a day or more to drive the same distance from point to point. Exploring the Book Cliffs from the air was like reading a book, Clay said, where each formation was like the page in a book. Rich coal beds could be easily traced for miles in a low flying airplane. The AEC and a few prospectors often did rim flying with sensitive radioactivity detecting devices, to prospect remote areas for radioactive uranium deposits, using a very low flying light airplane. As if to verify the truth of Jim's amazing exploits, Clay pointed out a set of aircraft pontoons hung stored in the rafters of the hanger, and told Jerry how Jim had used them to land on the swift flowing Green River in Desolation Canyon, where construction of an airstrip was impossible. It was thus possible to fly people and equipment into a prospector's camp at that inaccessible location.

Around ten o'clock Jim looked at his watch and said he had an early morning flight scheduled. Early morning, just at first light, is the best time to fly this desert terrain, especially in the warm months. In winter, morning fog could be a factor, but since the daylight hours were so short in mid-winter, early departures were routine for airplane pilots year round.

Next morning, breakfast at the Wayside Cafe had an entirely different clientele much to the travelers' relief. They then gassed up the Jeep and headed east on U.S. 6 & 50 toward Grand Junction. About 20 miles out, in a great barren flat with a single small gas station at the desolate junction, U.S. 160 branched off to the south toward Moab, their destination.

After they took the turn, Clay turned to Jerry. "Did you know this area, known as Crescent Junction, has deep deposits of potash, potassium chloride, used mostly as an ingredient in fertilizer? A Texas company I've done consulting for holds extensive government leases on thousands of acres from this point and toward the south. The thick potash beds lie at great depth, over a thousand feet deep, and were discovered by drilling. Someday my client hopes to open a commercial potash mine, like the Canadians have up in Saskatchewan. Wouldn't that be something?"

"Well, I knew thick salt and potash beds occurred all throughout this part of the Colorado Plateau, but I didn't know any of them had commercial possibilities," Jerry replied. "Just off to east, there," he continued, pointing, "is Arches National Monument, one of the most beautiful landscapes in the West, maybe in the entire world. A dirt road takes off to the east from this highway through a sandy wash, about five miles farther south. It's well worth a visit. I wouldn't want to try the Monument road in a passenger vehicle. You'd get stuck in the deep sand. There are so many sandstone arches it's difficult to count them. Big arches, little arches, double arches, more arches than you'd ever expect to see in one area. Too bad it's so hard to get to."

"Yeah," Clay said, "I've seen those arches both from the ground and the air, and it's like you say, very beautiful. Jim Hewitt and I flew this whole area, and also the Deadhorse Point area off to the southwest. It's all beautiful. Boy, when you're flying along just above the ground level up on the mesa, and then you whiz out over the two thousand foot high vertical cliffs at Deadhorse Point, your heart almost stops. To my mind, the view off Deadhorse Point down to the goosenecks of the Colorado River below, is prettier than anything at Grand Canyon down in Arizona. You know, they just made Deadhorse Point a State Park and they're building a road out to it."

"Yeah, and we're coming up on the most scenic part of the trip, to my way of reckoning," Jerry said. "Look over at the La Sal Mountains rising up out of the plateaus and canyons off to the southeast."

Blanketed with glistening white snow, the La Sals seemed much higher than they did in summer, a common optical illusion in mountain country. Just as Jerry said, it was a beautiful and relaxing scene off in the distance. They drove on in silence for a while.

The highway, which had been following a long and wide valley bounded on the west by a steep wall of red sandstone cliffs, now started a steep winding descent down to the Colorado River through crimson hued fluted sandstone cliffs and past mysterious side canyons. Off to the west, high on the slopes above the cliffs, numerous small tunnels and rock piles could be seen in the distinctive purplish and greenish beds of the Morrison formation. This colorful formation is host to many of the uranium deposits in this region, and it had been thoroughly prospected in recent years. Small tunnels and their waste dumps could be seen at intervals below the base of the cliff face and the softer marlstone slopes that formed the western side of the valley. These were old uranium prospects that never amounted to actual mines.

The highway finally emerged from the tributary side canyon it had descended and turned east up the river canyon. Just before the highway turned south onto the concrete bridge across the Colorado River, Clay slowed down as they passed a roadcut in a small anticlinal structure on the north side of the road.

"You see that outcropping?" he said to Jerry, pointing, "That's a small exposure of the tip of the uplifted Shinarump formation, and it's radioactive. Whenever a newcomer would come to Moab intent on becoming a uranium prospector, the town wags would send him with a geiger counter across the bridge to test the instrument. Invariably he would find this prominent outcrop and think he had discovered a uranium bonanza. I'll bet a hundred mining claims have been located by novice prospectors on that single roadcut," Clay laughed.

Moab was larger than Green River, but smaller than Price. It lay in a side valley that emptied into the main canyon of the Colorado River, forming a verdant cul-de-sac on the northwest flanks of the La Sal Mountains. Bare red colored sandstone cliffs and benches locally called slickrock bordered the valley in all directions, except to the south. The community began a short distance south of the Colorado River bridge and ran for a few blocks along the highway until the highway swept on to the south up arid Spanish Valley and over a ridge toward La Sal Junction and on to Monticello. Most of the Moab community lay right along the highway, and the residential area was east of the highway on shaded cross streets that seemed very pleasant in this barren country. Moab was an oasis, in every respect.

Clay turned east down one of the side streets through the small commercial center of the town and parked in front of the Trail Cafe diagonally across from the imposing Grand County Courthouse.

"I sure remember this place," Jerry said. "It's the social center of town. Isn't this Charlie Steen's favorite hangout?"

41

"Him and everybody else here," Clay said as they got out and went inside where a lunch crowd was gathering. The place wasn't as large as it looked and Clay was glad they had arrived before noon. He looked around and walked over to a middle aged man with a natty crewcut. "Well, I guess I knew where I'd find Big Dick Norman this time of day."

Startled, the man looked up and grinned. "Gosh, Clay, what brings you to town? Didn't our company check clear from that last job?" Clay sat down and motioned Jerry over. Clay introduced Jerry and Dick, an old client, and they ordered lunch.

Dick Norman was the local representative of the Texas potash company Clay had talked about. Dick lived in Moab and occupied a small office over a store on the highway that went through town. They went to Dick's office after lunch, Dick having picked up the tab.

On the way over, Dick pointed out shops and shopping facilities that had opened up recently, a mark of Moab's commercial growth and importance to the uranium mining industry. Dick told them about a big uranium mill planned for construction just above the Colorado River bridge on the other side of the river. Jerry wondered to himself if Dick was a member of the local Chamber of Commerce.

After seating themselves around Dick's large desk, he asked Clay, "Now, who are you working for this trip? Not our competition, I hope."

"Absolutely not," Clay said. "You know that I can't ethically work for your competition. I'm here on business totally unrelated to potash. I can't disclose my client or the nature of his business, but it has no conflict with anything you do. In particular, I'm looking for Howard Balling. Do you know where I can find him?"

"You bet. Howard is a fixture around here. He lives in a small house on the edge of town toward the Colorado River. I'll give you directions. What do you want to talk to Howard about?"

"I understand Howard is operating a gold placer mine on the Colorado River near Moab. I need to talk with him about prospecting alluvial deposits," Clay said. "I don't suppose you know anything about prospecting these kinds of deposits, do you?"

"Hell, I don't even know what you mean by alluvial prospecting, but I think you must mean Howard's gravel deposit just downstream from the bridge. The government withdrew sand and gravel deposits from location under the mining laws a few years ago. That decision almost put Howard out of the gravel business, until he figured out he could recover the fine placer gold in the gravel, call it a gold claim and keep on operating. He told me the gold recovery hardly breaks even, but he made lots of money selling gravel to local building contractors. Boy, he sure is good at twisting things around to his benefit. He has those government boys tied up in knots, thinking he's operating a gold mine when he's really operating his old sand and gravel deposit," Dick laughed.

Clay asked Dick if he had seen any of his old buddies from the USGS around Moab lately. Dick snorted. "Hell, this town is filled with USGS and AEC geologists. It seems their main purpose is to encourage newly arrived uranium prospectors to head for the most remote and impossible to reach places on the Colorado Plateau, all in the hope that someone will find something to encourage even newer arrivals to go to even greater lengths to find uranium deposits. I never saw such a well funded government program to entice non-miners to prospect and locate mining claims. It's no wonder so many poor fools come into town and then head out into the Canyon Country, never to be seen or heard from again. Most of them eventually get tired, and go back home to momma. But I'll bet the remains of some of them will eventually be found, dried out under some sandstone ledge back in a box canyon. I tell you, Clay, it's a disgrace what your buddies are doing to legitimate mining folks."

"Well, Dick," Clay said."You sound like you'd like some of that government attention yourself."

"Of course I would," he replied, smiling, "The potash industry could use a government guaranteed buying program, DMEA exploration loans, and high paid geologists and engineers coming around with free advice!" He paused. "Maybe not that last one, but the rest would be okay."

They talked a while longer about events in Moab and the tempo of uranium prospecting. After a while Dick and Clay ran out of conversation and stood up to leave. Clay and Jerry walked back to the Jeep and were about to get in and drive away, when Clay noticed some familiar faces staring at them through the cafe window. His heart missed a beat as he recognized the weathered faces of Lonnie and Willie Baker and their companion. Holy Mackerel, he thought, they've followed us. Without saying anything to Jerry, he got into the Jeep and drove to the nearby City Motel, his favorite stopping place in Moab. He registered them for the night, again sharing a single room to keep expenses down. Clay then told Jerry what he had seen at the cafe, and they speculated as to what it might mean.

It was now early afternoon, so they decided to look up Howard Balling. Following Dick's instructions, they had no trouble finding his house. There was an old pickup truck parked next to it and they knocked at the front door. A tall, lanky man in his 70s opened the door and peered at them.

"Mr. Balling?" Clay said. When the elderly man nodded, Clay continued, "My name is Clayton P. Greer, and this is Gerald Brooks. We're geologists from Salt Lake City and we'd like to ask you some questions about alluvial prospecting. Have you got a few minutes?"

"You boys aren't from the government, are you?" Balling replied, with concern in his voice. He seemed like a very intelligent and articulate man, just as he had been described to Clay.

"Oh, no, we're both private geologists about to embark on some alluvial prospecting and we were told you are an expert," Clay quickly answered. "We're not from the government. Dick Norman told us where to find you."

Balling relaxed and invited them in. The house was dim and cluttered with books, maps and papers. Pieces of driftwood and mineral specimens lined the mantle and filled several shelves. "What do you want to know about alluvial prospecting that you think I might know?" he said to Clay, as he peered intently at Jerry. "Don't I know you from somewhere?"

"Mr. Balling, I'm Jerry Brooks," Jerry said. "Back a few years ago I worked for the USGS out of Grand Junction. I met you then and you probably remember me from those days."

"Of course," Howard replied, smiling broadly. "I remember you well and I'm glad to see you again. You're looking fit. What are you doing now?"

Howard and Jerry exchanged pleasantries and swapped a few stories, and inquired about mutual acquaintances, as is the custom when mining men meet. It seemed they knew the same people and there were a lot of them. Clay sat quietly as the two older men talked on, enjoying themselves. He wondered how he was going to ask Mr. Balling all the right questions without revealing anything. Finally, Howard and Jerry reached a quiet moment in their conversation.

"Mr. Balling," Clay said, seizing the opportunity. "Jerry and I have been retained by a client who believes valuable gemstones can be found in the alluvial deposits of the Colorado Plateau. We are groping for a plan to investigate those possibilities, and a place to start. Can you give us any kind of pointers?"

An interested look came into Howard's eyes. "What kinds of gemstones?" he asked. Jerry nodded at Clay.

"Well, any and all kinds of gemstones, precious and semi-precious. Anything that will prove or disprove our client's theory," Clay said. "We're pretty sure there aren't any primary gemstone deposits in the sedimentary rocks of the Colorado Plateau."

"Oh, don't rule out the laccolithic intrusions that form the isolated mountains and ranges that dot the Colorado Plateau, like the La Sals, the Abajo Mountains, the Henry Mountains and Navajo Mountain. Those igneous masses could have reacted with sedimentary beds and created garnet deposits, for instance, and possibly other primary gem deposits." The gleam in Howard's eye showed he hadn't forgotten his geologic concepts, and could match jargon with anyone, even young geologists from the city.

Clay smiled. "That's where your vast experience comes in. In all your prospecting, have you ever encountered gemstones of any type in the Colorado River alluvial deposits? To your knowledge, has anyone?" Clay sat back, his heart racing.

Howard thought for a minute or two. "You've got me there. I've prospected placer deposits all up and down the Colorado River and most of its tributaries, and I've personally known practically everyone else who has done so too. I can't say any of us ever found anything that would qualify as a valuable gemstone, at least anything that was big enough for someone to cut and polish. Most of the alluvial materials in the Colorado River deposits are so small they can only be recognized under a hand lens. The coarse gravels in those alluvial deposits are mostly local rocks, intrusive rocks, chert and quartz. Minerals derived from igneous rocks are pretty rare, and, well, there is nothing that is even remotely like a gemstone. Your client is on the wrong track," he said.

"What about the placer gold in the Colorado River, where does it come from?" Jerry asked.

"The gold in the Colorado River is mighty fine, too. It comes from the west slope of the Rockies, but it is so reduced in size and flattened by the time it is transported down to Moab it's mighty hard to capture in a sluice or a gold pan. Why, down in Glen Canyon, near Hite, the gold is so small that it will float on the surface tension of water. I've seen tiny flecks of gold float right over the lip of the gold pan, too small to sink through the natural surface tension of the water. My placer deposit here at Moab runs only 50 cents worth of gold to the cubic yard of gravel and the gold isn't as fine as it is farther down the river. But if I didn't have a market for the gravel, I couldn't continue operations. Down in Glen Canyon, gold concentrations of 25 cents per yard are considered rich. I read somewhere that the gold in the lower stretches of the river is so small it takes 3,200 colors to equal one cents worth of gold. Why, that's about the smallest thing a man can see with the naked eye. Before my time here, back just after the turn of the century, a fellow named Edward Stanton surveyed a railroad down the main canyon of the Colorado River from Grand Junction to the Grand Canyon. His crews staked long placer mining claims the entire length of his proposed railroad, but those claims were never successfully mined, and most weren't even prospected. I think it was his scheme to tie up the federal land. The railroad wasn't built, either. It was all a crazy scheme. A few optimistic and determined old timers have tried to mine gold from the better gravel deposits on the river down in Glen Canyon, but none of them made any money. I think there was even an experimental gold dredge on Good Hope Bar, but it was a failure also."

"Howard, do you have any prospecting experience in the San Juan River?" Clay asked.

"I know there was a flurry of gold prospecting on the San Juan in the late 1890s, but I was never on that river. I can't think of anyone who was."

"Our client is convinced alluvial gemstones have been found in southeastern Utah, gems big enough to be cut and faceted. He thinks the source might be somewhere in the Rockies, maybe in the San Juan Mountains."

Howard couldn't give them any helpful information. He doubted if coarse gemstones were to be found in active alluvial deposits in any area that he knew about. He mused that certain ancient alluvial deposits might have been reworked by erosion, but he concluded, "Sorry, boys, I just don't have any advice for you."

"Can Jerry and I test out our prospecting equipment at your gravel operation?" Clay asked. "I'd like the opinion of an expert like you, and besides, we need the practice." In his mind, Clay wanted to see if any of the fine material in the Colorado River placers might be diamond fragments, something that might have gone undetected. Howard willingly agreed and gave them directions to his mining operation down by the river.

Clay thanked Howard and they headed for the door. Outside, Clay spotted a battered pickup truck parked in the shade of a tree, about a block away. He turned to Howard. "If anybody asks you about us, or why we were calling on you, don't say anything about gemstones. Tell them we were interested in the placer gold down in Glen Canyon." They left Howard standing in his doorway, waving warmly to them. Clay was careful to depart down a side street, so as not to pass the pickup parked down the road.

Back at their motel, Mrs. Sutton, wife of the motel owner, handed Clay a note. "Dick Norman called and left a message for you. He wants you to call that number." Clay thanked her and quickly went inside.

"Dick says his wife and family are in Salt Lake on a shopping trip and he's lonely," Clay said, coming back outside. "He wants to take us to dinner. You game?"

Jerry stopped rummaging around in the back of the Jeep, and said, "Have I ever turned down a free meal?"

At seven o'clock they drove over to meet Dick at the Red Rock Cafe, a new restaurant on the highway near the southern edge of town. Dick was already there, leaning over a table where four men were eating . When he saw them he broke away and came to greet them.

Picking a booth in the back, they ordered and sipped a round of beers Dick had arranged for before they arrived. "How did you know I drank beer?" Jerry asked.

Dick smiled. "For starters, I assume everybody from Utah is probably some kind of a Mormon. At lunch you had coffee, so I knew you weren't a tithing Mormon. In this dry climate Jack Mormons like beer. I just guessed."

Over a dinner of thick juicy steaks, Dick and Clay continued their earlier conversation about Moab characters and events. It had been six or seven years since Jerry had been in Moab, so he listened with interest.

"Since you left the area, the AEC has been promoting uranium prospecting something fierce. Like I told you earlier, it seems they want every school teacher, postman and shop keeper in the nation to be out there in the desert looking for uranium. Every week they arrange for newspaper and magazine articles to glamorize uranium prospecting. As a result, we get the weirdest people coming to Moab. I understand it's much worse over in Grand Junction. How is it in Salt Lake?"

"Well, in Salt Lake we get mostly uranium stock promoters. You know, guys who used to be horse traders and used car salesmen, folks who don't want to soil their hands with real work," Clay replied with a laugh.

Soon it was approaching 9:30 and Jerry felt tired. "I say we head back to the motel, old buddy," Jerry pleaded to Clay.

Dick decided to hang around the restaurant to visit with a couple sitting at a nearby table, so they thanked Dick for a great meal and left.

Back at the motel, just as they went inside, Jerry noticed the same dilapidated pickup truck Clay had seen earlier, this time parked at a lighted room just down the line.

Men operating a portable gold rocker.

5

BLANDING

The next morning as they were on their way to breakfast, Jerry noticed that the dilapidated pickup truck was gone. He told Clay what he had seen the evening before and Clay immediately went to the motel office. He returned with a broad smile on his face, informing Jerry that the Baker brothers had checked out early that morning and inquired about the motel closest to Hite Crossing at head of Glen Canyon on the Colorado River. Jerry and Clay both laughed, feeling glad to be rid of their stalkers.

"Just exactly how do you plan to prospect for diamonds down at Howard Balling's gravel mine?" Jerry asked Clay over breakfast at the Trail Cafe.

Clay explained that his research revealed that prospecting for alluvial diamonds was similar to prospecting for alluvial gold, but with some significant differences. Alluvial diamonds would stick to grease whereas any grease or oil would tend to cause small flakes of alluvial gold to float away on the surface of the water. Also, many diamonds were fluorescent under an ultraviolet light. He had tested Blaine George's diamond collection and they all fluoresced a distinctive bright blue, so any alluvial diamonds they found should be easily spotted under their ultraviolet lamps. At Clay's request Jerry had brought along both short-wave and long-wave portable ultraviolet lamps from his prospecting equipment inventory at the rock shop. Clay said he proposed to coat the lip of their gold pan with grease and rig up a blanket or something to block out the bright desert sunlight while they inspected the gold pan for anything that fluoresced. They both agreed they needed a good practical field exercise to work out any bugs.

After breakfast they headed down to Balling's gravel operation on the Colorado River, where they found Howard loading gravel into a rotating trommel with a front end loader. As they pulled up he dismounted and walked over to their Jeep.

"Right after you boys left, three guys drove up and questioned me about your visit. Just like you asked me, I told them you were interested in gold deposits down in Glen Canyon, below Hite Crossing."

"You did the right thing, Howard," Clay said, "Those guys are claim jumpers who have been following us all the way from Green River for the last two days. I saw their truck parked down the highway when we left your place, so I suspected they would come calling. Jerry and I were told this morning that those boys are headed for Hite Crossing, probably based on what you told them. By the time they figure out they've been misled, we'll be somewhere far away." They all chuckled.

With Howard watching curiously, Jerry and Clay set up the rocker on the gravel bar near the edge of the river and started shoveling gravel and pouring water through the device, alternating the shoveling and rocking. After a while Clay disassembled the riffles and put the concentrate into a gold pan. Squatting in the shallow water at the river's edge, Clay panned it down to about a cupful of black sand which contained several small flecks of gold. Clay then smeared some grease on the lip and swished the concentrate around and up onto the lip, but it did not appear that anything was sticking to the grease.

After briefly consulting with Jerry, Clay took the pan and both portable ultraviolet lamps and crawled under a large canvas that Jerry had extracted from the Jeep. Jerry joined him and they carefully inspected the concentrate under both ultraviolet lamps. While the greased area fluoresced brightly green, nothing else did. They consulted again, and decided to repeat the procedure at a different location. By then, Howard had returned to his gravel loading, shaking his head.

Again, all their work produced nothing. It was time to move on to the San Juan River. They said goodbye to Howard and drove back through Moab, continuing south down U.S. 160 to Monticello.

The drive took them through scenic Red Rock Country and eventually onto an eroded plateau. The highway branched at La Sal Junction, with State Highway 46 going east to Lisbon Valley and on to Naturita, Colorado. U.S. 160 continued south through more Red Rock Country, past Wilson Arch and onto a high plateau. This was the approximate route of the ancient Spanish Trail that meandered from Santa Fe in New Mexico, all the way to the missions in central California. In fact, the early Spanish travelers had crossed the Colorado River near Moab, which before the Mormons settled the valley had been known as Spanish Crossing.

They continued south along U.S. 160 to near Church Rock, an isolated round sandstone knob set in an open sagebrush valley. Church Rock was a prominent landmark where a dirt road branched to the west down a canyon and ran past Newspaper Rock. Newspaper Rock got its name from a dark stained sandstone cliff densely covered with ancient Indian petroglyphs, which was another prominent landmark. The dirt road past Newspaper Rock ended at the remote Dugout Ranch, about 15 miles beyond. Dugout Ranch was the last outpost on the edge of an immense wilderness called The Needles, dreaded even by airplane pilots who had to fly over this trackless region. A forced landing meant certain death, since rescue would be impossible.

South of Church Rock paved U.S. Highway 160 climbed onto a high flat tableland on the eastern flanks of the Abajo Mountains, sometimes locally known as the Blue Mountains. At an elevation of 7,000 feet above sea level, in country sometimes covered by snow at this late winter season, sat the very small community of Monticello. Monticello had an airstrip just north of the town and was the county seat of immense but empty San Juan County. Of even greater importance, it was the site of an AEC uranium ore buying station. Without the station it is doubtful the town could survive, since it barely survived with all of the business the AEC facility attracted. Except for the pinto bean farmers who had recently homesteaded the high arable tablelands east of Monticello, there was very little reason besides the county seat and the uranium ore buying station for the town to exist.

San Juan County was a hotbed of uranium claim staking, and the woman who served as the San Juan County Recorder was usually overwhelmed with mining claims. Clay recalled many a day spent trying to crowd into the small office to check ownership records. He also recalled that there wasn't a decent place to eat in the whole town. He, and most people working the county records, preferred to commute from Moab, or from Blanding, and pack a sack lunch to eat in the sunshine on the county courthouse steps.

Clay and Jerry drove through Monticello without stopping, continuing south on paved State Highway 47 toward the small Mormon community of Blanding. The narrow highway wound along the southeastern slopes of the Abajo

Mountains through sparsely timbered country for about 25 miles until it dropped into a pleasant valley in which the neat and orderly community of Blanding was located. Although small, Blanding was the principal town in southeastern Utah and a veritable oasis, like Moab. Clay recalled that only a few miles south of Blanding was the beginning of the long winding dirt road that ran west for about 100 miles to Hite Crossing on the Colorado River, at the head of Glen Canyon.

Holy Mackerel, Clay thought with a start, could it be that Blanding is "the nearest motel to Hite" where the Baker brothers were headed? Then he remembered that the tiny settlement of White Canyon, near the Happy Jack Uranium Mine, was only a few miles east of Hite Crossing and had a primitive rooming house that was better suited to the Baker brothers' taste. They surely would stay there. Still, he thought to himself, we'll need to keep a lookout for those rascals.

It was mid-afternoon when they reached Blanding. Clay drove directly to the town's cheapest motel incongruously called "King's Hotel" where he again booked a single room with two single beds. As he checked in, Clay asked the matronly woman behind the counter where he could find Charlie Nevilles, a boating guide. She took Clay to the door, pointed down the street and gave instructions. Then she showed Jerry and Clay to their room down one of two long halls in the one story U-shaped building that reminded Clay of a dormitory. Their room was sparse, but clean. A large bathroom down at the end of the hall served all guests in that wing. Their room didn't have a radio or a telephone but it was cheap, and favored by field crews and workers on a budget. Clay often stayed here when he was in town.

They drove down to find Charlie Nevilles, where they introduced themselves and asked if he was available to serve as their guide on a trip they planned down the San Juan River. Charlie asked them inside and they sat down in the living room around a large low table where Clay unrolled a map.

Charlie Nevilles was a compact man in his mid-forties, known as the master river runner of the San Juan River. Unlike other Colorado River guides of his time who used large World War II surplus rubber rafts and bridge pontoons, Charlie navigated the river in specially designed wooden dories, similar to the kind used by Major John Powell when he made the first explorations of the Green and Colorado Rivers in the 1870s. Charlie's dories were of an improved design created in the 1880s by Nathaniel Galloway, a Green River fur trapper. Galloway is also credited with inventing the modern method of river navigating, by pointing the boat upstream and appearing to row upstream so the rower could face downstream, moving slower than the current and steering around obstacles. In Powell's day the boats were rowed pointing downstream, leaving the rowers blind and causing the boats to race downstream faster than the current. Though ancient in design and carrying few passengers, Charlie's dories were more maneuverable than the huge pontoons or inflatable rubber rafts used by other river guides.

However, the small wooden dories might not prove as safe in extreme high water and big rapids. Early in the boating season the San Juan River should still be low and the rapids smaller. It was important for Clay and Jerry to float the San Juan while the water was low, so they could reach the gravel bars. Nevilles' small dories should permit them to navigate from gravel bar to gravel bar with frequent stops to take samples.

As they talked about their trip, Clay explained that they wanted to make frequent stops to take samples, but he didn't mention alluvial gemstones, letting Charlie think they were simply interested in placer gold. Clay asked Charlie to point out the prominent river bars and bench gravel deposits on his map.

It soon developed that their river trip would take nearly a full week at the least. Charlie had some scheduling conflicts since there was a small party of tourists arriving in about a week to take an early season run all the way down the San Juan to the Colorado River, getting out at the Crossing of the Fathers near Gunsight Butte and just above the Glen Canyon Dam construction site.

Charlie explained that nowadays *everybody* had to get out of Glen Canyon above the construction site since it was impossible to float the Colorado past the dam construction. Because of the unbroken steep canyon walls along the river, and the general lack of any other access to the river, the disembarkation point known as Crossing of the Fathers was the only getting-out place. It was the only place for many miles where the river could be approached from the inhabited west side, down Padre Canyon along a route discovered by a group of lost missionary fathers in the 1770s. This place could have been named Navajo Crossing because for more than a century Navajos had used this place to swim stolen horses and cattle across to their vast reservation when they returned from raids to the west and north.

It was now late in the afternoon and both Clay and Jerry were tired. Armed with information, Clay and Jerry decided to hunt up a place to eat dinner and to see if they could work themselves into Charlie's busy schedule. They agreed to meet again in the morning.

It soon appeared there was only a single eating place, aside from an ice cream parlor that also served hamburgers. Blanding didn't get many travelers who didn't bring their own supplies, it seemed, but Clay wasn't prepared to do his own cooking any sooner than he had to. He and Jerry would have plenty of opportunities to eat out of cans in the days to come. Convinced that the town offered nothing better, they parked in front of the tiny Town Cafe and entered.

Inside the cafe didn't look so bad, but it was empty. Clay and Jerry seated themselves at a table and waited. Soon a woman in her 40s appeared from the kitchen and handed them menus. "You're early. We don't get many customers until after dark."

"We're here for a few days," Clay said, "We're hoping to go down the San Juan with Charlie Nevilles. What looks good for dinner?"

She recommended the chicken fried steak and they chatted as she went back and forth from the kitchen. She was both the waitress and the cook. As they settled down to eat, an old man ambled through the door, looked hard at them, and seated himself at a nearby table. "I'll just have some coffee, Janie," he called out. She soon emerged from the kitchen with a large white mug and placed it before him.

He looked over at Clay and Jerry. "You fellows interested in Moki pots?"

"What's a Moki pot?" Jerry asked.

He studied them for a minute. "I thought you two were tourists, come to look for Indian things, old pottery and arrowheads, and the like. Sorry to bother you."

"Oh, don't apologize. I'm just not familiar with that term. What is a Moki pot?" Jerry said.

The old man warmed up and explained that Moki was a Mormon or Navajo term for the ancient Indians who predated the Navajos, and that Blanding was located on the eastern edge of a great area renowned for its ancient Moki dwellings and abundant Indian artifacts. In fact, he said, the abundance of Moki artifacts, and the demand by collectors and tourists, had spawned a local industry

54

digging for pots and artifacts. He told Jerry that most of the local folks had accumulated large personal collections, and several people made a good living exploring for and selling them, mostly pots and jars found in isolated cliff dwellings scattered over an area called Grand Gulch. He identified himself as Seth Shumway and said he was too old to dig, himself, but he knew lots of folks who did. Clay thought to himself, I'll bet he's a digger; I wonder why he feels obliged to deny it?

Shumway and Jerry then discussed these prehistoric Indians, how they lived a thousand years ago, where they might have come from, and where they eventually went. Shumway seemed convinced that the ancient Mokis had migrated all the way to central Mexico where they built the pyramids and temples near Mexico City, which were there when the Aztecs arrived even later. Jerry, on the other hand, thought the Mokis might be the ancestors of the Pueblo Indians of New Mexico who had moved to the south when there was a change in the climate.

Janie came to the kitchen door. "Those government people are determined to put a stop to all the pot hunting, so Seth Shumway you better learn to keep your mouth shut. You're going to get yourself and a lot of other folks in trouble. How do you know these men ain't from the government?" Seth stopped talking immediately, and sized up Clay and Jerry.

"Old timer, we're geologists exploring for minerals. We aren't government men here to catch local pot hunters. Anything you've said to us won't be repeated to anyone." Clay motioned to Jerry for them to leave, as he got up to settle their bill. They left Seth and Janie in a serious conversation at Seth's table.

Back in their room, Clay and Jerry spread out their maps and talked about their options for exploring, trying to prepare a plan that would match their needs, Charlie's schedule, and their client's budget. It was 10:30 before they finished, but Clay felt they now had a plan.

Next morning after breakfast at the cafe, they headed to Charlie Nevilles' house. Nancy Nevilles was busy getting their teenage children off to school, so Charlie, Clay and Jerry went over to a small outbuilding where Charlie had an office and stored his equipment. They cleared off a large work table and Clay spread out his map. After asking some questions about the schedule of his other clients, Clay laid out the plan he and Jerry had worked out.

Essentially, they proposed to join the tourist group on the early stages of the float down the San Juan, rather than wait for Charlie's return to Blanding after he dropped off the tourists down by Glen Canyon Dam. The tourist group was small, only six people, so Clay and Jerry could share a boat and stop off at pre-selected sites to take their samples, then catch up with the main group when they stopped for the night. Somewhere down the San Juan before it joined the Colorado, Clay and Jerry would leave the group and arrange for Jim Hewitt to fly them out. Charlie could either cache the boat or spread out the tourist group and take all the boats down to the final disembarkation point.

Charlie pondered their plan and looked over Clay's map. "I think it can work, but the logistics aren't exactly what you might think. First, I'll need a guide on each boat, to row and keep you greenhorns from swamping my boats. These boats will barely hold four people and their gear, and if you haul a lot of bulky extra gear as it looks like you will, the capacity of your boat will likely be only three people. I figure we'll need at least three boats and three guides. After you leave us, I can pull one passenger from each of the other two into your empty boat for the rest of the trip. My van and the trailer will haul nine passengers and all three boats back to Blanding, so I guess we can do it!" He looked up, smiling, "Can you fellows be ready to leave in five days?"

Clay was delighted. Charlie did some calculating, named a price for his services and Clay quickly agreed.

"I'll plan to be the guide on your boat, since you will need me to point out the gravel bars. Also, I want to be with you to keep you on schedule. I can't have you guys getting too far behind the others, not making it to camp each night. Distances and floating speed on the river can be mighty hard to judge. My assistants are good, but I don't trust them up against determined and strong willed guys like you. I'm the only one who can crack the whip. Besides, I'm mighty curious about what you're doing," Charlie said.

"Can I use your telephone to make a long distance call?" Clay asked.

"You bet," Charlie replied, "I'll just add the call to your bill. The kids should be gone to school by now. Use the phone in the house."

Referring to his notebook, Clay dialed a number and waited. "Oh, Hi Sandy, is Jim around? This is Clay Greer, calling from Blanding." "Jim," Clay said after a short wait, "how soon will your schedule allow you to fly down to Blanding and scout out a place to pick us up down on the San Juan River? It looks like the actual pickup will be April 7 or 8. Either of those days work for you?" There was another pause. "Sure, I know weather is the controlling factor but weather permitting, when can you fly down? I'm sure it won't take a full day to look over the country and pick a place to rendezvous. You probably already have a place in mind, maybe near Piute Farms down on the river. Isn't there an airstrip somewhere down there?"

After another pause, Clay exclaimed, "Wonderful! We'll be parked on the ramp at the Blanding airport by 9:30, waiting for you." He hung up the telephone and turned to Jerry, "Boy, are we in luck! Jim had a cancellation due to bad weather up north, so he can meet us in the morning. He has to fly back to Green River before dark but we shouldn't need him more than two or three hours."

Back at Charlie's office, Clay said, "We're in luck. Our pilot is coming down tomorrow and we'll pick a place for him to meet us in about two weeks. We think Piute Farms might be our getting out point, so I'll need you to tell us when we'll get there."

"Who is your pilot?" Charlie asked, looking up from the map.

"Jim Hewitt up in Green River," Clay said. "You know him?"

"Jim Hewitt is the very best," Charlie replied, "Everybody knows him. He's a legend. Maybe he can stick pontoons on his aircraft and land right beside us on the river."

"I doubt he will do that," Clay laughed. "We're going to check out an airstrip at Piute Farms, hopefully one near the river. Do you have information on the condition of any airstrip there? Jerry and I figure we will have checked out the possibilities on the San Juan well before we get that far down but upstream from there the river is in such a deep, narrow canyon that Jim won't be able to find any place to land."

"You're smart to scout out a pickup point," Charlie said, pointing to Clay's map. "Those hastily constructed bulldozer airstrips seldom last over a winter and a gully in the wrong place can wipe out an airplane. I've seen pilots successfully land on the dirt roads that crisscross the area around Piute Farms. You ought to check them out."

Next morning the skies were overcast, but the weather signs toward the Abajo Mountains and Elk Ridge looked good. After breakfast, Clay and Jerry drove a few miles south of Blanding along the paved highway to where the airport was located. It was near the point where the long dirt road branched off that went to Hite Crossing, 100 miles to the west. They walked around and looked at the several bush planes parked on the ramp and remarked how this airport must be the lifeblood for such a remote community. Precisely at 9:25 they heard an airplane engine and Clay spotted a high wing single engine Cessna 180 swooping down from Elk Ridge, right along a direct route from Green River up north. The Cessna circled the field and glided to a landing, taxing right up to them. Jim Hewitt cut the engine and climbed out.

Clay rolled out his map on the hood of the Jeep and pointed out where they wanted to fly. Jim studied the map a few minutes and motioned for them to climb aboard. Clay insisted on sitting in the rear seat where he could shift from one side of the plane to the other, and thus get an unobstructed view out either side as they flew along. Clay boarded first, then Jerry climbed into the right front seat and fastened himself with a seatbelt and a strap across the chest. He looked downright uncomfortable, his hands clasped in his lap. He stared at the instruments and gauges, then turned to Jim.

"I know you're a good pilot, Jim," Jerry said, "But what am I supposed to do?"

"Your job is to sit back, relax and look out the window. I'll do the everything." He then carefully folded and laid out an air navigation chart on his lap, making a few pencil marks. Jerry watched with interest.

Jim soon looked around, shouted "Contact!" in a loud voice and started the engine. Conversation was impossible. They taxied down the runway to the far end. Jim raced the engine, turned the key twice, as the engine seemed to falter and then roar back to life. He tapped the altimeter, adjusted it, looked all around to see if anyone was in the air lined up to land, then he aimed the airplane down the runway and raced toward the far end. About halfway down the runway the airplane was in the air.

Climbing to a few hundred feet, Jim banked left and departed toward the south, climbing above the paved highway below. Within a few minutes they spotted a small community, Bluff, on the north bank of the turbid San Juan River which flowed from east to west. Jim was at about 1,500 feet above the town when he banked sharply right and flew down the river, about level with the cliff tops to the north.

Clay reached up and tapped Jim on the shoulder, and asked him to fly just to the left of the centerline of the river so he and Jerry could see the river below out of the right side and spot likely looking gravel deposits in the bed of the river and on the benches and terraces on either side. Jerry leaned against the window looking intently down. It was an awesome perspective, just as Clay said.

The highway paralleled the river along its north bank for a short distance, then climbed up onto a bench and continued west quite a distance from the river canyon. Jim continued to follow the river channel, which here was the boundary between the vast Navajo reservation to the south, and empty federal lands to the north. Clay focused on the channel and the north bank of the river, since the south bank was Indian land and off limits for prospecting. They spotted numerous likely looking gravel bars in the river bed, and occasionally a prominent stranded gravel bar on a bench above the river representing an old river bar deposited before the river cut down to its present channel. Stranded gravel bars were excellent places to prospect for placer gold, so they must be good places to look for gemstones too, Clay thought. Clay and Jerry excitedly marked their maps and aerial photos so they could find these same spots later as they floated down the river.

Further down the river they spotted a narrow iron bridge spanning the San Juan River. Here the paved highway ended and the road passed over the bridge onto the Navajo reservation and ran southwesterly, eventually to Flagstaff in Arizona. The small riverside community of Mexican Hat, named after a bizarre rock formation, then came into view on the north bank. From this point downstream for hundreds of miles there were no other settlements on the San Juan or Colorado Rivers, until you got below Hoover Dam near Las Vegas. Jim continued to fly down the river, oblivious to the remote wilderness he was entering.

Not far below Mexican Hat they flew over the famous goosenecks of the San Juan, a renown place where the incised meanders of the San Juan River almost looped back upon themselves in narrow canyons hundreds of feet deep, where one loop of the river was separated by high cliffs from the next loop only a few hundred feet apart. Scenic aerial photographs of this marvel, and views from the high cliffs just to the north, had been made famous in travelogues and picture books, but to fly across the goosenecks just above the canyon rim was truly awesome. Jerry thought, in just a few days we'll be floating right through this very terrain. *I wonder what it will look like, from down there?*

It was hard to watch for gravel bars and take in the spectacular scenery at the same time, so Clay asked Jim to circle back so they could get a better look. This time they noticed there were few gravel deposits in the steep walled canyons. Below the goosenecks, the canyon of the San Juan became less meandering, but it was a lot deeper. Finally, they discovered that the canyon walls grew farther apart, and they found themselves at an open stretch of the San Juan River canyon, an uninhabited place shown on their map as Piute Farms. Apparently someone had considered this sandy expanse capable of being farmed. This was one of the few places where the lower San Juan River could be accessed by land.

Piute Farms was an incredibly remote place, approachable only from the south by a long, rough dirt road from the heart of the equally remote Navajo reservation. Isolated Navajo sheep herders and their families were the only seasonal inhabitants. Dirt rut roads seemed to run everywhere, and nowhere. Back in the 1890s during a placer gold frenzy on the San Juan River, a placer gold operation had been temporarily located at Piute Farms, but in the interval since then the area had lost what small population it once had, and returned to wilderness.

Jim descended and circled to get a closer look at the faint tracks in the sandy terrain down near the river. One long straight track, which looked like it might serve as an airstrip, attracted his attention. It ran along a low level bench parallel to the river, its shores heavily lined by willows, tamarisk and shrubs. Jim circled and swooped down parallel to it, only about 25 feet above the ground, for a better look. As he climbed higher, he turned to Clay and shouted, "I'm going to land. I want to walk it and chuck some rocks off. We'll need every inch of runway when I haul you out."

At 600 feet above the strip Jim made a wide circling approach. The ground rushed up to meet them as Jim applied flaps and slowed the aircraft to a dangerously slow ground speed. The Cessna 180 is a tail dragger, that is, it lands on its two main landing gear and drags its tail wheel in a high nose-up position. It can handle much rougher landing strips than airplanes with the newer tricycle landing gear just coming into prominence in the late 1950s, but once the tail wheel rests on the ground all forward visibility is very limited.

Jim kept the tail high for visibility. Jerry could see a gully across the strip at its near end, and felt Jim add power to keep the aircraft flying. Suddenly Jim raised the nose for landing, dumped full flaps and added more power. In an awkward nose high attitude the airplane wallowed in the air, glided over the gully which raced past Jerry's side window, and bumped to a rough landing squarely on the narrow sandy track. They didn't roll very far as the airplane came to a stop.

Jim cut the engine and opened the door to get out. Jerry emerged slowly followed by Clay. Jerry thought to himself, next time I'm going to select the rear seat. It looks a lot safer for a non-pilot like me.

As Jim and Clay headed down the sandy track, tossing rocks and sticks to either side, Jerry hiked down to the river's edge. Near the edge of the sandy beach between the water's edge and the willow and tamarisk fringe, he spotted the frame of a brush shelter or wickiup, probably built by Navajo sheepherders for shade the previous summer. It was bedraggled, with the leaves all dried and stripped away, but evidence of recent human habitation, nevertheless.

As Jerry climbed back up, Jim and Clay were just returning. He joined them at the airplane. "How does it look?" he asked.

"A little soft, but otherwise good," Jim replied. He reached inside and retrieved a small shovel from behind the airplane's rear seat. "Here," he said to Clay and Jerry, "Help me fill in the gully. It'll add several hundred feet to our runway, and we'll need it." They all walked back and started to shovel and kick loose sand and rocks into the depression. Soon they had it filled, Jim packed the shovel away and extracted a large canteen. "I don't fly these deserts without plenty of water, and some emergency supplies and a signal mirror," he said as he passed the canteen. "It can be an awful long walk out of some places, if you can walk."

Jerry thought to himself, what if we can't take off? Who knows where to look for us? How could we ever expect to walk to civilization from this remote place? It was a sobering thought.

Jim and Clay then lifted and pushed the tail of the airplane, turning it around. Jim laboriously taxied it back down the landing strip across the filled-in gully to the far end of the airstrip, while Clay and Jerry walked alongside. Again they turned the aircraft around and lined it up with the narrow sandy track. They all boarded, this time with Jerry in the rear seat, and Jim started the engine. Jim pulled up in his seat and peered over the cowling down the narrow track, then he carefully applied power until the heavy craft began to roll.

He added more power and the airplane lurched ahead, as he went to full throttle. Bumping down the runway, the fat wheels plowed through the deep sandy patches, and the tail finally lifted. From the rear seat Jerry couldn't see anything ahead, but he sensed that Jim's field of vision was now clear. With the tail elevated the airplane raced ahead faster, until Jim hoisted it into the air, leveling off a few feet above the runway while the airplane gained comfortable flying speed. Jerry heaved a sigh of relief to be airborne again.

Jim took a direct course back to the Blanding airport, a route which took them across the Grand Gulch area Seth Shumway had told them about. From the air the Moki dwellings nestled in the cliffs and ledges were practically invisible, but vehicle tracks and shallow diggings indicated where they were. Jerry spotted a lone pickup truck and two fellows looking up at them as they flew over, and suspected what they were up to. Far to the north loomed Elk Ridge and its distinctive landmark, the Bears Ears. Beyond Elk Ridge lay formidable Dark Canyon and the rugged wilderness called The Needles. These were little known regions, visited only by a handful of cowboys who tried to graze cattle in the remote hinterlands of southeastern Utah. The story was that most of the cattle released into this immense area never came out again. Nobody could find them, or drive them out.

Jim soon landed at the Blanding airport, which with its paved runway looked positively luxurious, and taxied up to Clay's Jeep parked next to the ramp. The only structure on the airport was a gas pump island, operated on the honor system. Jim topped off his fuel tanks, filled out a charge slip and placed it in a slotted metal box. They said their goodbyes and scrambled to the Jeep as Jim restarted the engine and taxied away in a swirl of dust.

With the entire afternoon before them, Clay turned to Jerry. "Let's take a side trip and see how far we can drive up to the top of Elk Ridge. We've got several hours 'til dark, and I don't relish hanging around the hotel." Soon they were headed west down the dirt road toward Hite.

After about seven miles, he turned north up Cottonwood Wash onto a much less traveled road. After another few miles a road branched off to the west and a small hand painted sign pointed to the Deer Flat Mine. Clay turned west and climbed up a ridge toward 9,000-foot high Elk Ridge looming ahead and to the north. They encountered snow banks but Clay was able to buck through. Finally they came to a high, almost flat rolling plateau scattered with pine and spruce trees. This was the famous ridge that dominated the northern horizon as seen from the communities of Blanding and Bluff. A layer of crusty snow on the road indicated that no one else had been on the ridge yet this season. Clay stopped the Jeep and got out to get his bearings. Jerry remained inside, since a cold wind was blowing out of the north.

Returning to the Jeep, Clay pulled out one of his maps.

After examining the map, Clay turned toward Jerry. "As much as I hate to, I think we ought to turn around and go back to Blanding. We're much too early in the season to go driving about on this snow cover. We'll wind up in a snow drifted gully, sure as hell. I was hoping to find someone at the mine, but there's nobody up here. What do you say?" Jerry quickly agreed, and they started back down the road they had fought so hard to drive up.

"Did I ever tell you the story of the Can of No Return ?" Clay said as they crept slowly down the steep wet dirt road. Jerry smiled and shook his head, knowing he was in for it. "Well," Clay said, "Two summers ago I was working out of Kanab, in a remote area east of the Paria River. The investigation area was on the west flanks of the Kaiparowits Plateau, a big high plateau sort of like Elk Ridge, only located west of the Colorado River. We were reconnoitering the head of Last Chance Creek and Croton Canyon, an immense roadless area that could be traveled only by driving the sandstone rims and then by heading up the bottom of the canyons. We figured it would take us four days to reach the headwaters of Croton Canyon, and then four more days to drive back out. If anything broke, it would be days before we could walk out. I knew from flying the area in the past that there were lots of dirt roads up on the flat top of Kaiparowits Plateau, which was right next to Croton Canyon, if we could just find a way to the top," he said, taking a breath.

"We calculated our fuel consumption, and filled the cargo portion of my Jeep station wagon with five-gallon G.I. gas cans. The can in the middle we marked with a red bandana tied to the handle. This was what we called the Can of No Return. If we had to use that can of fuel, it meant we had to turn around and drive out the same way we came in, or we would run out of fuel before we made it back. Well, it was mighty slow and tedious driving in, and we got mighty tired of camping out in those lonesome canyons. We couldn't even get radio reception on the Jeep radio at night, and there was no light to read by after dark. We drove the sandstone rims, filled in washouts, clambered over boulders and ledges, and had a hellava time just getting to our remote destination. The idea of driving out along the same route sure wasn't appealing. Finally we got to the base of the Kaiparowits Plateau looming 2,000 feet or more above us. We drove up Croton Canyon as far as we could possibly go, even winching up a 20-foot high nearly vertical ledge in the canyon floor, until we came to a 200-foot high box canyon. All the way up the canyon we had been scanning the slopes of Kaiparowits Plateau for some sign of a Jeep road or a dozer cut in the hillside, or any kind of a vehicle track on the mountain. We didn't see anything, and we were sick with disappointment."

Clay paused, thinking back on his experience. "We felt completely defeated as we turned back down the canyon, winching ourselves back down that 20-foot ledge, and slowly creeping down the canyon over boulders and ledges. I was driving and hanging out the driver's side window looking up at the steep sides of the plateau when I spotted the track of a bulldozer a few hundred feet up the hillside. There were no blade marks, mind you, just the track of the treads. I was determined to get out by way of the roads up on top of Kaiparowits, and I said to myself, that bulldozer certainly didn't come up this canyon, and somehow he got out to the top, so if a bulldozer can make it, by God, so can we. We turned straight up the slope and headed for that dozer track. We couldn't go anywhere but straight up, since to try to turn around would mean rolling the Jeep, it was so steep. When we reached the track, we followed it. After about three hours we reached the crest of the plateau, and followed the dozer track to a dirt road. At that point we knew we could make it out, so we pulled over and camped right on the spot. We felt so happy to be able to get KSL radio reception that night, and to know we wouldn't have to make that four day drive back through the canyons."

They were now almost to Blanding, but Clay's mind was still atop the Kaiparowits Plateau 100 miles to the west.

6

DOWN THE SAN JUAN

The next morning Clay and Jerry drove over to Charlie Nevilles' house and told him that Jim Hewitt had found a suitable landing strip at Piute Farms, so that was where they planned to leave the group. Charlie explained that he would provide their food and they only had to bring sleeping gear, clothing and personal items for the trip. But after he dropped them off at Piute Farms, they would be on their own until Hewitt picked them up.

Clay asked Charlie if he would be able to take the gold rocker on down the river in his boat after they parted company at Piute Farms, since the gold rocker wouldn't fit into Jim's airplane. Charlie went over to the Jeep and measured the rocker and agreed to deliver it back to Blanding.

Clay then asked Charlie to calculate the exact date when they would reach Piute Farms. Charlie consulted his maps and the calendar, and estimated that they should be there late on April 7. Jerry and Clay thanked him, and Clay asked to use Charlie's telephone to call to Jim Hewitt to schedule their rendezvous.

After confirming the date with Hewitt, they drove to Parley Redd Merchantile, a combination grocery/hardware store. As Clay pointed out to Jerry, their wait at Piute Farms might be extended if the weather was uncooperative. "You must always go prepared, and expect the unexpected in this remote country," Clay said as he purchased cans of beans, stew and fruit. Clay also purchased a dozen cans of condensed soup, "For the best instant lunch you could ever find," Clay said. "You'll see."

Clay then purchased a five gallon plastic jug to use as a water bottle, explaining, "We'll drink the river water, but it's so silty we'll have to let the silt settle out before we can drink it."

"Geez," Jerry said, "This is enough food to feed two people for over a week. What if Jim arrives on schedule? How will we ever get all this junk into the airplane?"

"Well," Clay replied, "We can always leave what we can't take out as a present for the Navajo sheepherders who roam that area." They hauled their supplies back to the motel room, where it filled one duffle bag.

"Janie, are there any non-Mormons in Blanding?" Clay asked Janie that evening as they were having dinner.

Janie paused and thought for a moment. "No, I don't think there are," she replied, "Unless you count the uranium prospectors up on Elk Ridge. I think some of them might be. Those guys could be anything."

"How come this town is all Mormon? How did the Mormons come to settle this area so completely, when it is so isolated from the rest of Mormondom in Utah?" Jerry asked.

"That's a real story, the most miraculous story in the history of the Mormon Church," she said with excitement in her voice. "Back in the late 1870s the Mormon Church selected several families living in southern Utah and ordered them to migrate to southeastern Utah and colonize the region. Those families never hesitated, and loaded all their belongings into wagons and headed east. About 90 miles east of Escalante they came to the brink of Glen Canyon on the Colorado River. The river ran deep at the base of a vertical cliff, more than a thousand feet below. The only break in those cliffs was a narrow cleft which came to be called Hole in the Rock. Well, those faithful Mormons built a narrow trail down through that cleft, dismantled their wagons and lowered them by ropes down to the river, led their families and livestock down the trail, then they floated across the river, reassembled their wagons and continued east across the slickrock country and trackless desert until they finally came to where the town of Bluff is now located. They were so worn out by then they couldn't go any further, so they settled there. As Bluff slowly grew, and after some other Mormons joined them from down in Old Mexico around 1900, some of them moved north to this more hospitable valley and they settled Blanding in 1903. Until recently I don't think anybody knew this remote Mormon colony even existed, leastwise it didn't seem that anybody in Salt Lake cared," she concluded with a snort.

As she was talking two locals came in, and they nodded in agreement as she finished.

As Janie went back to the kitchen, Clay turned to the men and remarked, "Janie tells us there are still uranium prospectors up on Elk Ridge. Do either of you know if the Deer Flat Mine is still operating?"

The younger of the two replied, "Yep, the Deer Flat Mine is still operating, and so are a few other mines and prospects. But, you know, Elk Ridge is buried under snowbanks this early in the year. I doubt if anybody is actually up there. Those fellows usually winter in Cortez. Are you folks uranium prospectors?"

Clay identified himself as a consulting geologist from Salt Lake City and introduced Jerry as his field assistant. The two men introduced themselves as Art Shumway and Chester Cox, local farmers in town to meet Charlie Nevilles on business.

"You two must be our river guides," Clay said and told them that he and Jerry would be passengers on the trip down the San Juan. He invited them to sit at their table and have a slice of Janie's pie while they waited for Charlie. It turned out Art was Seth Shumway's nephew, and after they loosened up over a glass of milk and a slice of pie, they admitted to being pot hunters and diggers for Indian artifacts too. In fact, Charlie had asked them to guide this particular group of tourists, since those folks wanted to make a side trip into Grand Gulch to see the ancient Indian ruins.

"We Mormons have always referred to the early Indians as Moki, but not so long ago some university people came here to dig in the ruins, and they called the Mokis by a new name, Anasazi. When I asked them, they said Anasazi was the Navajo name for Ancient Ones, meaning the inhabitants before the Navajos arrived. I guess the terms Moki and Anasazi mean the same," Art said.

"You're absolutely correct," Clay said. "The term Moqui is an old Spanish word for the prehistoric Indians down in northern Arizona, near Grand Canyon, so I suspect the Mormon term derives from the old Spanish term. I think the two terms are interchangeable."

"What can you guys tell us about all the rock art and drawings we see on the canyon walls in this region? Sometimes they're called petroglyphs and sometimes pictographs. Tell me, what is the difference? I admit to being confused." Jerry was looking at Art as he asked the last question.

"All the rock art around here is supposed to be the work of the ancient Moki indians," Art replied, "Except the modern drawings showing modern figures, like horses and rifles. Those are believed to be the work of modern Navajos, or maybe bored cowboys." Chester was nodding in agreement, so Art continued,

"The term pictographs refers to painted drawings, made with mineral pigments and clay dabbed on the surface of the rock. They don't last very long except in caves and under big ledges. Petroglyphs are drawings pecked and chipped into a rock surface, allowing the lighter sandstone to show through the dark desert varnish coating on boulders and cliffs. Those drawings are permanent and far more common." He paused, then asked Jerry, "Do you know what desert varnish is?"

"You bet," Jerry replied, "That's the iron and manganese oxide stained surface of really old sandstone boulders and cliffs. Over many years the stain leaches out of the sandstone, and makes an ideal dark surface for scratching and carving." Looking over at Art, he asked, "I don't suppose you know what all those rock art symbols mean, do you?"

"Well, not exactly," Art said. "The animals and stick figures are thought to represent good luck for hunting expeditions, and some of the grotesque figures are believed to be Moki medicine men and demons. Some folks think the abstract geometrical symbols point out the location of water holes and food caches hidden nearby. Me, I'm not so sure."

Just then Charlie Nevilles came through the door.

"Well, I see you boys have met each other. That's good," he said. "Art, Chester, these are the river prospectors I told you about." When Charlie heard that Clay and Jerry were asking about uranium prospectors on Elk Ridge, he turned to Clay. "Have you ever been up on top?" Clay nodded and Charlie continued, "Those tall ponderosa pines up on the north side of Elk Ridge are the most beautiful trees I've ever seen. And the overlooks down into the head of Dark Canyon are awesome. Art, here, knows that country well. He claims to have been all the way down to the mouth of Dark Canyon where it empties into Cataract Canyon on the Colorado River, above Hite Crossing. Of course, since everybody knows you can't get back out of there, I don't believe him."

Clay was impressed, and peppered Art with questions about the route he had followed, what he saw, and how he eventually got back. Art described his adventure as a vast labyrinth of steep canyons, high cliffs and shadowy glens, with numerous untouched ancient cliff dwellings probably never before seen by modern eyes. He told how their small party of five local young men finally reached the Colorado River and constructed a raft of driftwood logs and scraps of the rope they had used to descend Dark Canyon, and floated down to Hite Crossing. The ferry operator, Art Chaffin, sent word back to Blanding and relatives came to fetch them. My God, Clay thought, this guy should write a book.

Charlie then explained that Art and Chester would be bunking at his house for the next two days, helping him get everything ready. He turned to Clay. "What are you guys doing tomorrow? You need to be ready to leave the next day, so don't plan anything."

"We've finished all of our shopping. I was thinking we might drive down to the San Juan River at Bluff and try out our gold rocker on the gravels there."

"That's a good plan," Charlie said. "You should plan to leave your vehicle at my place while we're on the river. My wife can pick you up at the airport when you fly back."

As they were all leaving, Clay asked Charlie, "Who does the cooking on the river?"

"I do," Chester said. "I'm a good river cook, and Charlie supplies only the best grub. You'll like it."

Back in their room, Clay kidded that they might miss the Town Cafe's home style cooking. "Well, I'm ready for a change. I hear these float trippers eat pretty good," Jerry replied.

The next morning they got off to a late start and drove the 75 miles south on the paved highway to Bluff. "I sure can see why those early Mormons relocated to Blanding as quick as they could," Jerry remarked as Clay drove slowly through the settlement looking for a suitable place to get down to the river. "There ain't much room to farm in these river bottoms, and except for the river there don't seem to be anything here. Those Mormon colonizers Janie spoke about must have been plumb wore out to have stopped here in the first place."

Clay soon spotted a rut road down to the river's edge and headed down. Getting out and looking around, he selected a gravel bar in the bed of the river, and a good stranded gravel bar on a ledge just above the highway. While Jerry assembled the rocker out on the river bar, Clay drove back up to the highway to the edge of the gravel bench. He shoveled about six cubic feet of prime looking material into large canvas bags and loaded them into the back of the Jeep. By the time he got back, Jerry had the rocker assembled and was ready go.

Clay suggested they eat a "field lunch" before they started and handed Jerry a can of condensed Scotch Broth soup, a GI pocket can opener, and a spoon. They ate the contents cold right out of the can. It was quite filling and tasted a lot better than it looked.

Remembering what Clay had said when they were shopping, Jerry had to admit cold canned soup was convenient, compact and tasty.

After their break Clay looked around the river bar, selected the best looking place to dig and dragged the rocker over to a spot between the excavation and the water's edge. He shoveled and poured water while Jerry vigorously shook the rocker. Clay tried to measure about six cubic feet of gravel into the hopper before he asked Jerry to stop. He then lifted the riffles out and raked the concentrate into a gold pan, almost filling it.

Setting the pan down, he unloaded the canvas bags he had filled earlier and dragged them over. They repeated the process, pouring the contents into the hopper as, this time, Clay did the shaking. Rotation of these duties was to mark the rocker operation for the rest of the trip.

When the contents of the canvas bags had been put through, Clay again removed the riffles and raked the concentrate into another pan. Then, side by side, they squatted at the river's edge and reduced each pan down to less than a cupful of concentrate. By then the winter sun was getting low, and it was getting cold. They decided to head back to Blanding and their motel room to inspect their results under the ultraviolet lamps.

Before they left, Clay headed to the single gas pump in town and gassed up. Clay then asked the attendant if he could leave the rocker in his work shed overnight, and pick it up tomorrow. The man agreed and they pulled it down. Clay thought, I'm glad to have it off the roof. It attracts too much attention everywhere we go, and that's something we don't want.

By the time they got to Blanding it had been dark for some time so they drove directly to the Town Cafe for their "Last Supper" as Clay put it. To their surprise the cafe was full of customers and they took the last empty table and sat down. Janie was dashing about, taking orders and refilling coffee mugs, but she had a helper in the kitchen, cooking up a storm. As Janie approached with menus, Jerry asked, "Where did all these people come from?"

"I told you most of our business comes in after dark. You boys always ate earlier. Of course, this crowd is a mite bigger than usual." She rushed off before Jerry could say anything further. Come from where? he thought.

Clay and Jerry looked around, wondering if any river-running tourists might be among the crowd. Some of the hungry patrons were obviously truck drivers with rigs parked just outside. Others looked like tradesmen, maybe salesmen passing through. Two tables were couples, possibly tourists, but Clay couldn't spot a group of six anywhere. As some customers left, Jerry got a chance to question Janie.

"Where the heck did all those folks come from?" he said. "What did you mean when you said this happens regularly?"

"Just travelers. Some come down from up north," she replied, "headed to Kayenta, Tuba City or Cameron, in Arizona, on the way to Grand Canyon or maybe Flagstaff. Some come up from those towns, headed to Moab or Cortez. A few even drive in from Hite Crossing, headed east or north. It seems they all want to drive as late as they can, but soon after it gets dark they stop here to eat. I suppose that those who pass through before it gets dark decide to just keep going, to the next place to get a meal. It happens this way 'most every night." She looked at the dwindling crowd. "The local folks never come in. They all eat at home."

Back at the motel, Clay and Jerry took their gold pans down to the large bathroom at the end of the hall, closed the door, turned off the lights and inspected the concentrates under both ultraviolet lamps, first the long-wave lamp, then the short-wave. Clay let out a whoop. "Hot Damn, look at this pan Jerry! See those little blue flecks? Those are diamond fragments!" Jerry discovered a small blue fleck in his pan, too. They were both ecstatic, realizing that diamonds, even if they were only tiny fragments, had been found in the San Juan River gravels. Where there are fragments, Clay reasoned, there were bound to be larger stones. Their alluvial prospecting strategy was working.

Back in their room, they picked out the fluorescent fragments and inspected them carefully under a hand lens. Jerry wished he had brought along his binocular stereo microscope to get a better view, as Clay placed one the specks between two small glass plates and slid them around. The tiny diamond immediately gouged the smooth glass, confirming the extreme hardness of their tiny specimen. Clay then smeared a thin coat of lubricating grease on a piece of glass and washed the diamond fragments carefully across the grease coated surface. Sure enough, the fluorescent fragments stuck firmly, and couldn't be flushed away with vigorous washing. The test worked, just as the books said it would.

Clay put the samples away and consulted his notebook and the small scraps of paper he had placed in each pan to identify its location. He determined that the sample containing the most fragments came from the bench gravel deposit and the other sample came from the gravel bar in the river bed. Clay figured the place where the diamonds accumulated was near bedrock rather than distributed throughout the gravel bars in the river.

Two very excited men went to bed that night, anxious to get onto the river in the morning and explore for real diamonds, as Jerry expressed it. Clay was confident that bigger gravel samples would have yielded more evidence of diamonds, and perhaps a respectable sized stone. He planned to telephone Blaine George in the morning to report their results.

They were up early the next morning and packed their personal gear, equipment and supplies into the back of the Jeep, and made arrangements with the motel owner to store their extra belongings until they returned. They then had a quick breakfast at the Town Cafe and drove over to Charlie Nevilles' house.

The double decker boat trailer was already loaded with three dories and numerous coolers and supplies. Jerry discovered that there was plenty of room for the rocker they had left in Bluff the evening before. The tourists hadn't arrived yet. They transferred their load into the trailer as Charlie went inside to answer a telephone call.

"Well, that was from our guests," he said when he returned. "They're in Cortez, Colorado, and won't arrive for another three hours so we won't be able to launch 'til after noon."

Clay took this opportunity to call Blaine George with the news. George asked how their budget was holding up and promised to make a deposit into Clay's bank account to cover their expenses so far.

Clay then telephoned his office to check messages and asked Jeanie to telephone Jerry's wife to tell her everything was going smoothly, and that Jerry would call her when they got off the river in a few days.

Jerry and the guides were swapping tales when Clay returned to the trailer. Clay joined them, telling Jerry that all was well at home. It should be nice drifting down the San Juan in a boat if the warm weather continued, he thought to himself.

Just before noon a big Pontiac station wagon with Colorado license plates pulled into Charlie's side yard near the boat trailer. As the doors popped open, out poured six young women dressed in blue jeans, tight fitting capri pants and long sleeved shirts, some wearing hiking boots and all obviously intent upon an outdoor adventure.

Clay, Jerry, Art and Chester stood gaping in silence, as Charlie walked over to greet them and Nancy came to the door.

"Well, ladies," Charlie said, "I'm glad you made it."

Charlie turned to Art and Chester. "Boys, help the ladies load their belongings. And ladies, meet Clay Greer and Jerry Brooks. They're geologists from Salt Lake City who will be going part way down with us, looking for mineral deposits."

Eying Clay and Jerry with mild interest, the women smiled and introduced themselves. The driver and apparently the leader of the group was Patty Brotherson of Denver. Next was strikingly pretty Sandy Logan, also of Denver. Wendy Smithers and Sarah Phipps were both from Boulder, Colorado. Then came June Browning from Golden, Colorado, who was Sarah's younger sister, and finally Carol Koch from Littleton, Colorado, who appeared to be the oldest of the group and who was identified as a "writer/journalist" along to document their trip.

They were all close to the same age, ranging from the late 20s to the mid- or late 30s, and outdoorsy looking. Apparently they had traveled together as a group before. In addition to this river trip, they planned a day long side trip into the lower reaches of Grand Gulch on the way down. This is going to be a most interesting trip, Clay thought to himself.

Nancy Nevilles then called them all into the house for sandwiches, and the travel weary ladies first took turns washing up. Because there was little room inside, the men took their sandwiches and drinks outside and ate lounging around the boat trailer.

After lunch everyone assembled at the van which looked like it might once have been a small school bus. It barely accommodated the 11 river trippers and Nancy Nevilles, who would drive it and the empty trailer back to Blanding. Charlie had hired a local man to make the long roundabout drive to Crossing of the Fathers via Lees Ferry in Arizona to meet them and bring the boaters back.

The return trip would be a long drive, indeed, and almost as much a testament to their stamina as the float trip.

The trip to Bluff in the crowded van was long, but uneventful. When they arrived Clay asked Charlie to stop at the gas pump so they could retrieve the rocker. Then Charlie backtracked to the rut road down to the river's edge. He backed the trailer to the water's edge and the men heaved the dories in, tying the boats to the trailer. Charlie carefully supervised the loading of each dory. Bedding, tents and food were placed in large rubberized bags to keep them dry, while cooking utensils, lanterns and fuel were stored in bow compartments of the various boats. Life jackets were handed out, with instruction to always wear them while on the water. Finally the long oars were untied and mounted. They would be their sole power and Clay noticed that there was a spare oar for each dory.

Charlie then placed Art and three of the young women into one dory, Chester and the other three women into the second, and Clay and Jerry with their bulky rocker into the last one. He said goodbye to his wife, stepped into the third dory and they were off. The three guides took up their oars immediately and turned the pointed bow of each dory upstream, so the guide faced downstream where he could oversee their route. The dory's position was controlled by rowing upstream and calculating downstream drift in the moving current. By means of hard rowing the dory's drift could be halted and made to sit motionless in a gentle current. It was almost impossible to row upstream except in slack waters.

Just below the launch site they encountered their first riffles and standing waves which the dories navigated stern first with the guide slowing the descent by vigorously rowing upstream. It was smooth and exhilarating, and Clay could hear the women oohhing from the other boats.

Clay sat in the stern, sharing the broad benchlike seat with the rocker. From there he could see past Charlie in the middle seat with his oars, who faced him, and past Jerry in the narrower front bench, also facing him. Facing upstream Clay watched as Nancy Nevilles waved goodbye and returned to the van, heading back to Blanding.

Soon Bluff community disappeared behind a bend in the river and a grove of cottonwood trees and they were alone on the river. Clay twisted himself around to look downstream but his bulky lifejacket and the rocker prevented that. He would need to face the stern next time, or he would again see the whole river trip backwards. He noticed that the two women seated next to each other on the wide rear bench of the other dories had shifted around and were facing downstream.

Clay asked Jerry to be on the lookout for any good gravel bench that they ought to sample, since he couldn't. Before long Jerry gestured and pointed ahead. Clay turned and spotted a prominent low bench covered with coarse gravel. He motioned for Charlie to head for it. Charlie called out to Art and Chester to take it slow and wait somewhere below while his boat stopped to investigate. Clay realized Charlie had no idea what their sampling procedure involved and how long it would take.

"Jerry," Clay said, "We'll need to set up and load the rocker in record time and pan the concentrate later, maybe tonight in camp." Jerry nodded.

As soon as Clay felt the dory touch shore, he quickly shoved the rocker onto the beach, grabbed a shovel and three large canvas bags and rushed over to the gravel deposit. Motioning Jerry to position the rocker, he shoveled furiously to fill some canvas bags about half full, a total of about eight cubic feet. Jerry rushed up and dragged the first bag down to the rocker, while Clay dragged the second. Charlie dragged the third bag down as Clay loaded the hopper and poured water while Jerry vigorously shook the rocker. Within 15 minutes the bags were emptied and Clay removed the riffle and poured the concentrate into a small linen sample bag. Before Clay had closed the bag, Jerry and Charlie were already loading the rocker back on the dory. Jerry quickly took his seat, Charlie assumed his seat at the oars, and Clay pushed off and climbed onto the stern seat, this time facing backwards.

The entire operation, from landing to departure, had taken less than 30 minutes, but the other boats were now far downstream and out of sight. They would get really far behind if they stopped often to take samples. Well, so be it, Clay thought to himself. We came to take samples, not to enjoy ourselves.

They stopped three more times, taking seven or eight cubic foot samples at the best looking deposits, some on river bars and some on bench deposits. As dusk approached and the air began to get cold, they spotted a blazing fire on the north bank and angled toward their party's camp. Art and Chester had pitched four small tents, and a gasoline lantern was burning brightly. As they landed they could smell something good cooking.

Chester said that dinner wouldn't be ready for another half hour, so Clay decided he and Jerry should pan down the concentrates while there was still some light. They panned furiously and were just trudging back to the campfire, tired and wet, when Chester called out, "Chow's on!" Both Clay and Jerry were almost too tired to eat, as they sat on the sandy beach while Chester, assisted by Art and Charlie, dished out grilled T-bone steaks, baked potatoes in aluminum foil, hot baked bread and canned peaches. Everyone ate in silence for a while, then the women began to talk among themselves, and one of them played softly on a harmonica. Soon they were singing, and the men just sat listening, and digesting their big meal. Chester, who was still messing around with a large cast iron dutch oven, called out,"Who wants some pineapple upside-down cake?" Clay decided that Jerry was right, "Those float trippers eat pretty good."

Before Clay and Jerry turned in for the night, they checked their concentrates under the ultraviolet lamp. All showed tiny fluorescent diamond fragments, but all were about the same size as their first samples taken the previous day at Bluff. Clay was discouraged that the diamonds were so small and so few, since the gravel samples taken today were larger. Where were the larger stones?

Clay and Jerry unrolled their sleeping bags in their tent. The women shared two tents and the guides were in the fourth. Clay's bag was a GI surplus feather-filled mummy bag, while Jerry's was a larger rectangular shaped civilian flannel-lined bag. In addition, Jerry carried a flannel sheet to stuff into cold corners and plug up the large opening in his bag, on cold nights. Clay, the seasoned field man, slept on a rubberized ground cloth directly on the ground. Jerry, older and wiser, had a well used rubber air mattress that was flat by dawn. In the morning when Clay peeked out of the tent he observed a very cold Charlie sipping hot coffee from an enameled steel mug, standing by a blazing campfire. Clay pulled on his cold stiff field clothes from the day before and joined him. Charlie handed him a mug and poured some black coffee, all without a word.

"Charlie," Clay said, breaking the silence, "We need to have a better plan for taking samples today. Jerry and I can't rush and work so hard, and we need to take larger samples. Maybe we could start out earlier than the rest, let them pass us during the day, and then we'll catch up with them in the evening. That way we can spend more time taking samples and not get too far behind. How about it?"

"That oughta work," Charlie replied, "Chester has a big meal planned for tonight, so he will want to make camp early, and the ladies will probably want to delay launching until the sun is well up and it's warmer. I heard two of them say they wanted to take a swim." Charlie smiled broadly. "Can you imagine that, swimming in this cold muddy water?" After a pause, he added, "Our camp tonight will be about ten miles below the bridge at Mexican Hat. How many samples do you figure you'll be taking today?"

Clay quickly looked over his maps and aerial photographs, and said that he wanted to sample two large bench deposits they had spotted from the air, one upstream from Mexican Hat and the other a few miles below the bridge. He estimated that they would probably take as many as six. I really want to take large samples at those two deposits, because they look like the best on the river," he said.

When Jerry joined them Clay told him about their plans. They then ate a hasty breakfast and were on the river before the women had gotten up.

They stopped and took quick samples at several locations, concentrated the samples in the rocker and moved on. At the first big bench gravel deposit on Clay's map they took an enormous sample, almost two cubic yards, and ran it through the rocker. Charlie pitched in, working the rocker and shoveling gravel. They joked that they were a three-man mining operation. The concentrate from this operation filled five of Clay's small sample bags.

Opposite the mouth of Chinle Wash there were small rapids in the river caused by an accumulation of outwash debris from the side canyon. At this season, before late Spring runoff from the mountains upstream, these rapids were small and easily navigated. But in periods of high runoff, these rapids could be monstrous standing waves, and running such swift and high rapids would be like riding a rollercoaster, and possibly dangerous in their small dories. On the other hand, extreme low runoff could leave jagged rocks exposed in the river, which could puncture boats and rafts. There were no waterfalls or ledges in this stretch of the San Juan or along the Colorado River in Glen Canyon.

Their next landmark was the bridge across the river at Mexican Hat on the north bank of the river. Mexican Hat got its name from a prominent stone pillar in the bluffs just north of the community. The soft sandstone and marl of the slender pillar was topped by a flat ledge of erosion resistant sandstone, forming a protruding circular capstone somewhat resembling in profile a Mariachi sombrero. Hence the picturesque name.

They passed under the steel trusses of the bridge shortly after stopping for lunch, and continued drifting in the muddy current. They were busily working on their second large deposit when the other two boats drifted past. They exchanged greetings, and Clay observed that the women were now dressed in shorts and halter tops, soaking up the warm sun. He felt he was missing out on some fraternizing, but such is the life of the working man, he thought to himself.

Later in the afternoon they sampled a promising river bar right in the middle of the channel where small ledges in the bedrock formed natural riffles in the stream, almost exactly like the riffles in the rocker. Clay was very excited, figuring this location was like a giant rocker, one that had operated for centuries. If diamonds couldn't be found here, then there weren't any.

Well before sunset they arrived at camp with campfires blazing and their fellow travelers lounging on large driftwood logs near the water's edge. Pleased with the work they had accomplished and their timing, they landed the dory and started to unload. Art greeted them, and one of the women, pretty Sandy Logan, came over and offered an icy gin and tonic in a large paper cup. What a nice way to end the day, Clay thought.

Chester was preparing a large beef roast in the dutch oven, and he served hors d'oeuvres and cold beer as they waited for it to cook. Patty Brotherson, the group leader, had supplied the gin and tonic mixer, which Clay much preferred over the "Utah" beer. Jerry and Charlie, on the other hand, preferred the beer. Utah beer contains a maximum of 3.2% alcohol, whereas "strong beer" contains up to 6% alcohol. Beer lovers claim the difference in taste is great. Utah law prohibits the sale of beer containing more than 3.2% alcohol, which requires beer distributors to water down beer for sale in Utah, hence the name. The conventional wisdom is that only Jack Mormons can develop a liking for Utah beer.

Clay was beginning to relax and feel comfortable, but he knew he couldn't allow that. They still had several sample bags of rocker concentrate to pan, and the sun was still up and warm. He motioned to Jerry, and they both trudged down to the dory and retrieved their pans. Nearly an hour later they had just finished pouring the last gold pan concentrate into its glass vial, when Chester shouted, "Chow's on!"

Clay wondered how Charlie was able to bring so many delicacies on such a long river trip. When asked, Charlie pointed to the huge coolers and explained that the cool weather permitted him to refrigerate fresh supplies for a longer time than was possible in the hot summer. He added, "We'll have to resort to canned supplies toward the end of this trip."

"Tomorrow," he continued, addressing the whole group, "We'll be passing through the famous Goosenecks of the San Juan. Down here in the channel you can't appreciate the way the river winds around unless you pay close attention to the frequent changes in direction. Up on top it's quite another matter. Tomorrow night we should reach the mouth of Grand Gulch where we'll camp for two nights to allow you to visit the ancient Indian ruins in the lower part of the canyon." Turning to Clay, he said, "The following night we should reach Piute Farms where Mr. Greer and Mr. Brooks will be leaving us." He sat down as Chester served up a peach cobbler.

Several of the women seemed disappointed that Clay and Jerry would be leaving them, "Before we get to really know you", as Sandy Logan said. Clay enjoyed the attention, but recognized it as mere innocent flirting.

Later, at the river's edge in the dark, Clay and Jerry poured each vial of concentrate back into the pan, sloshed it around, and inspected it under the ultraviolet lamp. Clay was astonished to find that the concentrates from the huge samples taken on the promising looking bench gravel deposits contained only a very few tiny diamond fragments. He was appalled when the most promising sample taken from the natural riffles in the river channel itself contained no flecks of diamond at all. It was a disturbing development, and it could mean only one thing: they were going away from the source of the diamonds!

That evening a south wind came up, a precursor of a major change in the weather. Clay had a very uneasy feeling as he drifted off to sleep.

Wooden dory on the San Juan River

7

ESCAPE FROM THE SAN JUAN

All night the south wind blew, increasing toward dawn. Clay slept fitfully, waking several times during the night as the gusting wind rained sand down on their tent from the nearby cliffs, coating everything. At first light Clay pulled on his field clothes and unzipped the front fly of the tent. Outside Charlie was already standing by the campfire, which was swirling in the wind.

Charlie motioned to the large coffee pot at the upwind edge of the campfire and handed Clay an enamel mug. Clay poured himself some coffee and stood silently observing the windswept camp. The other guides were still hunkered down in their bedrolls, hoping the wind would die down.

"Charlie," Clay said, "Jerry and I have a change of plans. We need to go back up river. The samples we took yesterday clearly indicate that the source of the minerals we're searching for are somewhere upstream, not in the bed of the river itself. How far is it back to Mexican Hat?"

Charlie looked upstream for a moment, and replied, "Well, it's probably only 15 miles or so by river, but it might as well be 100. You can't row against that current, and it ain't possible to hike up the river canyon to Mexican Hat. It ain't even possible to climb out of this canyon, and if you could, there's no roads. The nearest road out would be at the Goosenecks Overlook a few miles further downstream, but you can't climb out of the canyon there either. I'd say you boys are in a mighty bad place to suddenly decide you want to go back."

Clay and Charlie then explored every possibility either of them could think of, but there simply was no practical way back to Mexican Hat, or anywhere for that matter. When they went under the bridge at Mexican Hat, they passed the point of no return until they reached Piute Farms. If Clay and Jerry rushed down to there, they would have to wait days for their pilot to pick them up. They were stuck.

By now Jerry had joined them. When he heard the prognosis, he shrugged. "I guess we'll just have to relax and enjoy the float trip for the next few days." Looking over at Clay, he added, "I suppose you'll want to continue sampling the best bars along the way, just to confirm your conclusion." Clay hadn't thought that far ahead, but he nodded.

"You aren't likely to run across any good deposits until we get well past the Goosenecks, so I recommend we stick together until you spot a good place," Charlie said, turning to observe another whirlwind marching up the sandy shore. "This is going to be one hellava day on the river. We need to get started, wind or no wind."

Charlie rousted out his guests and the crew, fed them a gritty breakfast and broke camp. They were soon on their way over occasional rapids as the winds blew sand and pebbles from the cliffs above, coating them and the equipment with dust and grit. They could hardly look up at the cliffs along certain stretches of the canyon, the grit was so bad. After a while the river canyon straightened as before, and Charlie announced they had passed through the renowned Goosenecks. On such a miserable, dusty day, the passage was anticlimactic. Clay and Jerry were glad they had seen the Goosenecks from above. The tourists were probably unaware of what they were missing.

Twice Clay had Charlie stop for samples, but these were small and the anticipation of discovering diamonds was gone. Clay and Jerry panned the rocker concentrates right on the spot and examined them by ultraviolet lamp under a sheet of canvas. Neither sample showed any signs of diamonds, not even small fragments. Nevertheless, Clay stored the panned concentrates in small glass vials, and labeled each to show where the sample had been taken.

Toward late afternoon the south wind reached a crescendo and they felt it shift to out of the northwest, marking the passage of a cold front. Dark clouds filled the sky and the temperature dropped by about 15 degrees within an hour. Rain now threatened, and where the canyon walls were lower they could see rain clouds over Elk Ridge to the north. Camp tonight would probably be a wet experience. I hope this weather clears out by day-after-tomorrow when Jim is due, Clay thought to himself.

This was the first day that Clay and Jerry had stayed with the other two boats. Clay noticed how chummy the women had become with their guides. "Do you ever worry about these ladies getting too chummy with your guides?" Clay asked Charlie. "Are either Art or Chester married?"

"Hell, Clay, this is mild!" Charlie replied. "Every unattached young woman on a float trip develops a crush on her guide, especially if he's young and good looking. My boys are good Mormons and, yes, both are married with small children. They ain't about to get involved with these gentile women, no matter how hard they might try. Of course, these girls are all experienced travelers, and they watch each other pretty close, to keep anything too serious from developing. I think all of those ladies, except Sandy Logan there, are married and not about to do anything foolish. Them ladies are just enjoying themselves, sort of like guys do when they get out." He paused, then asked, "You ain't married are you? You want me to set you up with Sandy? She's unattached, and the youngest and prettiest of the whole bunch!" He laughed, and Clay stuttered his decline of the offer. "That writer, Carol Koch, would like a little love interest for the magazine article she's writing. If you and Sandy were to strike it off, this adventure would be complete in her view. You sure you don't want me to set you up?"

"Charlie, do you ever take groups on land trips into this canyon country?" Clay asked, changing the subject abruptly.

"You bet," Charlie replied, "I like to take my guests on four-wheel safaris into Grand Gulch, up onto Elk Ridge and down to Natural Bridges National Monument. I've taken groups over to Four Corners and Monument Valley on the Navajo reservation, even over to Hovenweep and Mesa Verde National Park in Colorado. Of course, most of my summer guests want to do the float trip down the San Juan early in the summer and down the Colorado River in late summer. That doesn't leave much time for backcountry trips but if I get a request, I try to do it if my schedule allows me."

"Many of your guests want to visit the Navajo Indian Reservation?" Clay asked.

"Well, the Navajo Nation doesn't exactly welcome tourists. There isn't any nice place to eat or stay, and the tribe prohibits whites from conducting commercial activities on the reservation. Camping by non-Indians ain't allowed. Someday maybe the reservation may open up, but for now about the only way to see it is to find some accommodations outside the reservation, or in the few indian communities along the way. All my outings have been short day trips."

It was nearing dusk when Charlie announced that the mouth of Grand Gulch Canyon was just ahead, and they would be putting ashore on the north bank to make camp. They would camp here for two nights, while the tourist party went to see some of the Moki Indian ruins in the lower part of Grand Gulch Canyon. Tomorrow looked like it would be a long day. The evening of the following day would see them at Piute Farms, where Clay and Jerry would be left off for pick up by airplane the following morning. Clay was in a quandary as to what to do on the day the tourists hiked into Grand Gulch. It looked like it would be completely wasted for him and Jerry.

Art and Chester quickly busied themselves pitching tents and preparing the evening meal. The weather was threatening, with large rain drops starting to fall. Charlie pulled the dories far up on the shore and tied them securely. Jerry unloaded the rocker and dragged it up to their tent. Clay asked what Jerry had in mind. "I been thinking," he replied. "If our pilot flies us out, the first thing we'll want to do back in Blanding is prospect upstream on the San Juan. We'll need this rocker, and we won't be able to wait for Charlie to float it down to the gettin' out place, and then drive it back to Blanding. That would take nearly two weeks. So I decided to see if this contraption can be disassembled and flown out with us."

Clay agreed. If they were very careful, Jerry figured they could separate it into parts and back in Blanding, where they had access to hardware and parts, Jerry was confident he could reassemble it as good as new. Their work was set out for them; they would spend the next day dismantling the rocker.

Clay and Jerry then wandered outside to see what was happening. Down on the river bank Art had rigged up several fishing lines in a small embayment of the river. Jerry approached and asked what he was fishing for.

"Catfish," he replied. "The best eating fish in the world. Have you ever had catfish from the San Juan?"

Jerry admitted he had never tasted catfish, from anywhere. He preferred mountain trout. Art pulled in his first catch, a one-pound slimy flatheaded wriggling beast with a sharp spine protruding from its back. After he had landed a half dozen, all about the same size, he took the string up to Chester's cooking table to clean them, and before long the aroma of the deep fried catfish spread over the camp. Chester served hors d'oeuvres of sliced fillets of deep fried catfish, fresh from the river. The ladies raved, and Jerry reluctantly took a taste. He agreed with

Art that catfish tasted every bit as good as trout. He even finished off a batch of leftovers.

The rain held off, and soon Chester called out, "Chow's on!" The entree tonight was a baked meatloaf.

Around the blazing campfire after dinner Sarah Phipps broke out a flask of fruit brandy. Art and Chester didn't imbibe, but you'd never suspect it from their behavior. Clay noticed that Charlie and Jerry sampled the brandy, but mostly drank beer cooled in the river. The women were soon singing campfire songs, a pleasant end to a long and windy day on the river.

During the night it rained, but the dawn was crisp and clear. A light south wind came up as the hikers started into Grand Gulch Canyon after breakfast, suggesting another storm might be on the way. Charlie had decided to join the hiking party, which left Clay and Jerry alone to carefully disassemble the rocker. Jerry, under Clay's supervision, was successful and the task was completed by mid-afternoon.

Since the hikers weren't expected back until nearly dusk, Jerry decided to try his hand at fishing for catfish. Using Art's primitive equipment, and following the instructions Art had given him, Jerry had a string of 15 catfish by the time the hikers returned. This time he watched the cleaning process intently, aiming to master all phases of catfishing.

The women were completely exhausted, but eager to tell Clay and Jerry about their observations and discoveries. Art had shown them three Indian mummies stuffed with some of their belongings into burial ledges where the dry climate had preserved them over the centuries. They left everything undisturbed, but Clay wondered how long that would last. They entered intact cliff houses containing whole pots and other household items left as if the inhabitants intended to return. And they also saw sites where pot hunters had dug up the area and removed who-knows-what. Everyone considered the long hike a great success.

After snacking on more catfish hors d'oeuvres, courtesy of Jerry Brooks the proud fisherman and Chester Cox the master cook, washed down by beer and pop chilled in the cold water of the river, the crowd enjoyed a beef roast and diced potatoes Chester had left in aluminum foil slowly cooking in a fire pit while they hiked. The women were too tired to sing campfire songs that evening and everyone retired early.

During the night the south wind increased, and by morning rain was threatening. Breakfast was a hasty affair, sprinkled with sand and dust from the swirling winds. Their camp area was more open than the deep canyon of the upper river, and this south wind seemed much stronger. After about two hours on the river the wind shifted to the northwest, bringing a heavy rain. Even draped in ponchos it was impossible for the passengers and crew to stay dry in the open boats, and the float down the slowly moving river soon became a miserable experience. Near lunchtime they reached Piute Farms and Clay spotted the landing strip where Jim Hewitt had landed the previous week. He motioned Charlie to pull to the south shore and let them off. It was raining harder than ever now, so they made it quick and the other boats swept by with only timid waves of goodbye from under drenched ponchos. Charlie wished them luck and pushed off, rowing strongly to catch up with the other boats.

Clay and Jerry were now completely alone on the rainy south bank of the San Juan River, a great empty area. Their sudden and complete solitude came as a shock. Jerry suggested they throw a canvas sheet over the skeleton of a wickiup nearby. It was the only possible shelter in sight, so they quickly unpacked a large canvas sheet and stretched it over the stick frame and dragged their belongings inside. Placing another small canvas on the wet sand, they evaluated their miserable situation.

Since the entrance to the wickiup faced east, and the wind and rain were from the northwest, Clay decided that a small campfire opposite the entrance might help them dry out and provide warmth that evening. Clay and Jerry quickly gathered some driftwood and started a fire. Jerry, old Boy Scout that he was, built a log reflector behind the fire to direct some of the heat into the wickiup. It worked, and soon they were starting to dry out. They felt sorry for the folks out in the open boats, who still had several hours before they reached their camp for the night.

Nightfall came and the rain continued. The hastily erected canvas sheet leaked in a few places, but they located their sleeping bags in dry spots and avoided getting wet. As an extra precaution, they covered their sleeping bags and duffle bags with scraps of canvas. For dinner Clay punctured the lid of a can of stew and placed it at the edge of the campfire. When it was warm, he opened it with a GI can opener and offered it to Jerry, along with an opened can of peaches. After

86

their skimpy but nourishing meal, they turned in.

At first light Clay rolled over and peered out. There was only a drizzle but the clouds were low and solid. Jim Hewitt could never fly in on such a bad day. The campfire was smoldering, so Clay added some dry twigs from the wickiup frame and fanned the coals into flame. Jerry began to stir, and as they both lay in their sleeping bags they tried to decide what to do. Jerry offered to go catfishing to supplement their canned fare and also to avoid boredom. Clay decided to check out the airstrip and see if they had any neighbors.

But first they had a breakfast of canned soup, again warmed in the campfire.

Then while Jerry rigged his fishing pole with a hook, line and sinker donated by Art Shumway, Clay carried the five-gallon plastic jug down to the river and filled it with river water. Jerry had saved a lump of gristle from his can of stew from the night before, and now he carefully cut it into three small fish baits. "To think, this small scrap is all that stands between us and boring canned meals," Jerry said in mock dismay. Clay wished him luck, poured off a measure of clear river water into his canteen from the jug, and headed up to inspect the airstrip.

The heavy rain had opened up the gully he and Jim had repaired last week, and created still another. Hauling sticks and small rocks, he filled both gullies, noticing the wet sandy soil was more compact than the dry sand, which should make a better runway for the airplane when it was time to take off. Satisfied that the airstrip was in as good a shape as he could make it, Clay looked around to see if he could spot any signs of human life.

About a quarter mile to the south near a clump of cottonwood trees, Clay spotted a high mound of dirt. He thought it might be a Navajo hogan and as he approached he could see that it was unoccupied, but still in good shape. This structure followed the traditional pattern. From the outside it appeared to be a huge dome-shaped mound of dirt, piled about seven feet high and about 15 or 20 feet in diameter at the base. A doorway on the east side was the only opening, except for a smoke hole at the apex. Inside, as Clay's eyes adjusted to the dim light, he could see that the structure was made of tilted rough cedar posts about eight feet long, laid against a double framework of much larger cedar poles erected in the rough form of a multi-sided box. The outer lower frame was roughly hexagonal, while the inner taller frame was a square. The outer shell of cedar poles and posts forming the side walls were inclined inward only slightly from the vertical, whereas the poles lining the domed roof were laid at more of an angle to form an inclined roof almost in the shape of a dome.

All the posts and poles in the walls and roof were covered with smaller sticks and branches, over which a foot or so of dirt had been piled to seal out moisture and light. The inside floor had been excavated down about two feet, giving a high vaulted feeling to the interior, considering the outside dimensions of the structure. In the center, directly under the smoke hole in the domed roof, was a fireplace for cooking and heating in winter. Since there was little evidence of a fire in the fireplace, Clay figured this hogan was used during the summer months as a place of retreat from the desert heat. It didn't look like it had been occupied for months, perhaps longer.

Navajos live in widely dispersed single family habitations Clay recalled, seldom closer than a mile apart, so this unoccupied permanent hogan strongly suggested that no one else lived nearby. For some cultural reason, the entrance to every Navajo habitation faces due east, to catch the rising sun. Even their temporary brush wickiup had the entrance facing due east. Clay considered moving their camp to this more substantial structure, but decided against it. There might be mice, snakes and fleas living in the dark recesses of the log walls and, after all, their canvas covered wickiup was sufficient. And it was closer to the river and right next to the airstrip.

Clay then hiked back by a roundabout route, looking for signs of occupancy. He saw only signs of livestock herding in the area, sheep and goat dung, and old campfire rings left by the herders. Back at the wickiup, Jerry was still fishing.

"How's the fishing?" he asked as he joined him at the river. Jerry gave him a thumbs up, and pointed to a string of fish tied to a stake at the water's edge. Clay counted five moderate sized catfish on the string, to which Jerry was about to add a sixth.

"How can you catch six fish on only three baits?" Clay asked.

"These babies will eat anything. I lost two of my precious baits before I landed the first one, who took my third bait, so I cut out his guts and used that as bait to catch the others. Catfish innards make better bait than canned beef gristle, anyhow."

"You better slow down, or we'll have more fish than we can handle," Clay said. "How do you plan to cook these beauties?"

"I thought I'd try broiling one or two on a stick by the campfire. I don't know how they will taste, but maybe we can try some for lunch. It's getting about that time."

Clay poked around in the smoldering campfire and raked a bed of coals off to one side. Jerry then rigged some forked twigs to hold the spits over the coals and placed the two fish to simmer slowly, turning them frequently. Clay unpacked two cans of soup and placed them on top of his duffle, just in case. Before long the aroma of the cooking fish told them their plan was working.

Jerry soon laid the fish on a paper plate, removed the willow spits and carefully peeled away the skin. "Dig in," he said and Clay peeled a large white fillet from one fish, and tasted it. "Maestro, I salute you," he said, bowing. It turned out that one catfish apiece made for a hearty lunch, and Clay saved the canned soups for another time. The five-gallon jug of river water had settled out completely by now, leaving a two-inch layer of silty sludge in the bottom. The remaining water was crystal clear, so Clay carefully poured it into canteens. He rinsed out the jug and filled it to start a new batch.

"What do we do, now?" Jerry said, as they finished lunch.

"Wait for the weather to lift," Clay replied.

"I think I'll go do some more fishing," Jerry said. "I want to try baking some catfish in clay, and we'll need more fish for breakfast anyway."

By mid-afternoon the rain had stopped and the clouds were clearing from the north. Clay was reading and Jerry was still fishing when there was the drone of an engine in the distance. Clay jumped up and looked northward. A speck appeared above the horizon and quickly took the form of a silver Cessna 180. Good old Jim Hewitt circled overhead, cut his engine and started a wide circling glide to land. In a long straight-in final approach he added power and put the airplane in a nose high very slow powered descent. It seemed to come in fast, flared just two feet above the ground before touching down, planted its wheels firmly on the dirt strip and rolled to a stop. The left side door popped open and a tall familiar figure climbed out and waved.

"I'll bet you were worried about this weather and all," Jim said, smiling. He shook Clay's hand and looked around. "Where is your partner?"

Clay explained that Jerry had become addicted to catfish fishing and was getting in his last precious moments. He walked Jim down to their camp and they started hauling sleeping bags, duffles and the dismantled rocker up to the plane where Jerry joined them. Clay and Jerry folded the canvas sheet and sorted out what to leave behind for the Navajo sheepherders.

"While you guys sort things out, I'm going to hike down to the far end of the airstrip to do a little constructin'," Jim said. "We'll need every inch of runway to haul us and all this gear into the sky. It's a good thing I didn't top off the tanks back in Monticello while I waited for the weather to lift." He reached into a compartment behind the rear seat and retrieved his shovel and headed off down toward the far end of the airstrip.

When he returned about forty-five minutes later, Clay and Jerry had piled their gear beside the airplane. They piled the excess gear as a gift to the Navajo sheepherders, marked by a tall pole covered with strips of fluorescent plastic flagging sure to attract their attention. "You boys help me turn this airplane around before we load up, and please empty that water bag and all your canteens before you load them," Jim said.

They wheeled the airplane around and Jim carefully loaded the gear, strapping the dismantled rocker into a rear seat next to where Jerry would sit.

Clay and Jerry walked alongside the airplane as Jim taxied back to the takeoff end of the narrow airstrip. Then all three of them pushed the loaded airplane around, until it was aimed straight down the runway. Jim did his routine check under the engine cowling, walked slowly around inspecting the propeller, control surfaces and tires, and then ordered them aboard.

Before he started the engine, he turned and told Clay that he had constructed a dirt hump at the very far end of the runway, to bounce them into the air if they weren't already airborne by then. Clay nodded solemnly, and Jim shouted, "Clear!" and started the engine. He cycled the propeller twice, revved the engine to check the magnetos, noted that he had good oil pressure, tapped the altimeter, noted the compass heading and slowly advanced the throttle. The airplane shuttered and slowly started to move.

Jim continued to add power and now the airplane was taxing ahead slowly, then faster and faster. Finally the tail came up and Jim could see over the engine cowling. Kicking hard on the rudder pedals, he kept the airplane aligned with the narrow airstrip as it laboriously plowed ahead. Looking to the rear over one shoulder, Jerry could see a giant plume of sand and dust swirled up by the churning propeller. It seemed the heavy airplane wasn't going to fly, but they sped faster and faster down the runway. Clay could see the sagebrush and low willows at the far end of the runway approaching fast. The airplane was perceptibly lighter, but still not ready to fly as they came to the very end of the runway and bounced off the end, into the air. The engine roared and the airplane picked up speed as it became free of the ground. Jim kept the nose down as they sped over the sagebrush a few feet below, struggling for flying speed. Suddenly the airplane swept out over the river, twenty feet or so below, and Jim nudged the nose a bit lower to pick up more speed. He headed up the river, just above the surface of the water, gradually picking up airspeed. Clay could see the constricted canyon walls a mile or so ahead, and looked apprehensively at Jim. Finally the airplane climbed a bit, and started a shallow turn to the left, until it was lined up downstream, still climbing slowly. Only then did Clay and Jerry dare taking a breath.

Jim slowly reached altitude and took a bearing upstream toward Blanding. Clay leaned over and told Jim they wanted to fly past Bluff so he and Jerry could inspect the San Juan River channel. They needed to scout access points to the river channel to find ways to drive down to the river. Jim nodded and flew a direct course that took them just north of Muley Point and the Goosenecks Overlook. Looking down, they got another fantastic view of the Goosenecks of the San Juan.

As Bluff came into view it became apparent that upstream from the town there wasn't any road access down to the river. East of Recapture Creek Jim pointed out a prominent dirt road coming down from the north across a mesa that stopped at a dry stream bed that Clay identified on his map as Montezuma Creek, which also marked the western boundary of the Aneth Extension to the Navajo Indian Reservation. Apparently the county had built a road right up to the reservation boundary, but stopped there. However, it looked as if you could drive down the dry creek bed to where it emptied into the river. A maze of faint trails ran from the end of the government road eastward toward the small Navajo community of Aneth located farther east and right on the north bank of the river. Flying farther eastward, they could make out many dirt trails and some new roads in the vicinity of Aneth, some going down to the river. It looked from the air as if small construction projects dotted the landscape east and northeast of the community. From Aneth a good dirt road ran eastward along the north bank of the river.

Satisfied that they had seen everything they could from the air, Jim headed back toward Blanding along the prominent dirt road he had spotted earlier. They could see that it connected to State Highway 47 about halfway between Blanding and Bluff.

Landing, Clay used a public telephone mounted on a power pole to call Nancy Nevilles. Clay and Jerry unloaded their gear, Jim fueled his airplane and, since dusk was approaching, said his goodbye and took off for Green River hoping to land there before dark. Clay and Jerry sat on their pile of sleeping bags and duffle until Nancy drove up just as the sun set in the clearing western sky. They figured Jim would be landing at about the same time in Green River, far to the north.

On the drive to Blanding Clay filled Nancy in on the trip and asked her to stop by the King Hotel so they could arrange for a room. By the time they reached the Nevilles' house and transferred their gear to the Jeep, it was dark. They turned down an invitation to dinner with Nancy and her children, and headed to the Town Cafe. As they parked out front, Jerry pulled out his long string of catfish and carried them inside.

As they entered, Janie looked up and did a double take at Jerry's long string of fish. "What in the world have you got there?" she asked, smiling.

"Our dinner, my dear, if you'll cook it for us," Jerry replied.

"You'll have to clean them, 'cause I don't clean catfish. Come back to the kitchen, I think I can find a hammer and nails, and a pair of pliers." Jerry looked surprised, but followed her. As they went through the kitchen door, Clay looked around and halted in his tracks. There at a corner table sat Lonnie Baker, alone this time, staring at him. Clay pretended not to recognize him and sat down at a table in the far corner of the cafe, picked up a discarded newspaper, and pretended to read it.

After a few minutes Lonnie got up, went over to the kitchen door, said something to Janie, walked to the cash register and plunked down some money, and left. Clay eased up and peered out the glass pane in the front door. Lonnie got into his pickup and drove off to the south. Clay hurried to the kitchen to tell Jerry what he had seen.

92

There, under Janie's supervision, Jerry had nailed the head of each cat-fish to a wooden table, and was cutting and peeling away the skins using pliers to grasp the skin just behind the catfish's head. It was a sight to behold, but a slick way to skin these slippery beasts. Clay didn't have the heart to interrupt such an enterprise, so he went back to his table.

When Jerry joined him, while Janie cooked the fish, Clay informed Jerry what had happened, and they speculated about what it meant. Janie soon joined them in a catfish feast that helped dispel the uneasiness the sight of Lonnie Baker had caused.

Cessna 180 struggling to take off on a dirt land strip.

8

HATCH TRADING POST

The next morning, as Clay and Jerry left the King Hotel to shop for hardware and supplies to reassemble the rocker, Clay spotted the pickup he associated with the Baker brothers parked at the back of the hotel's dirt parking lot. Asking Jerry to wait, Clay went back inside and spoke to the woman behind the desk, Maude Gibbs.

As they drove into town, Clay filled Jerry in. "Lonnie has been in town asking about us. His brother and the others are still in White Canyon, but apparently they've figured out that there isn't any gold to be mined from the Colorado River. Lonnie has been asking all around town, 'Where did they go?' Do you think we should tell him?"

They laughed at their private joke, and determined to work out a plan to send the Baker brothers on another wild goose chase.

Meanwhile, they found what they needed at a small farm supply store, and returned to the hotel parking lot to work on the rocker. Jerry soon had the rocker back as good as before.

Just then Clay caught a glimpse of Lonnie Baker peering at them from a window in the hotel. Pretending not to see him, Clay said in a loud voice to Jerry, "Well, now than we've got the damned thing fixed, let's get back to Piute Farms as quick as we can. It's a long drive to Piute Farms and I don't want to lose another minute." They put the rocker on the roof of the Jeep and while Jerry tied it on, Clay went in and explained to Mrs. Gibbs where Piute Farms was on the map, pointing out the roads to take to drive there if anybody asked where they went. He was virtually inviting the Baker brothers to visit them at Piute Farms, if Lonnie asked the predictable questions to get an explanation of what he had just overheard.

As Clay and Jerry drove away, they could see Lonnie deep in conversation with Maude Gibbs.

About 15 miles south of Blanding they found Utah State Highway 262, a new gravel road that headed east toward Montezuma Creek and Hatch Trading Post. About seven miles down the highway turned southeast toward Montezuma Creek, while a smaller dirt road ran due east to Hatch Trading Post. Clay and Jerry continued southeast until the road ended abruptly at Montezuma Creek. A sign announced that they were at the boundary of the Navajo Indian Reservation. Numerous tire tracks led south down the dry creek bed, so they followed them as far as the Jeep could go. When they could go no farther, they parked the Jeep and hiked the short distance down to the north bank of the San Juan River.

Clay soon spotted a large gravel deposit on a low sandstone bench just downstream from the mouth of Montezuma Creek, an ideal place to take a sample. Upstream were other deposits that could also be sampled. He and Jerry then returned to the Jeep, untied the rocker and hauled it down to the deposit. Clay took a large sample, about nine cubic feet, and washed it through the rocker at the river's edge. While Jerry retrieved the ultraviolet lamp and a sheet of canvas from the Jeep, Clay carefully panned the rocker concentrate down to less than a cupful.

"Goddammit, Jerry, we've hit the Mother Lode!" he exclaimed as he looked at the sample under the lamp. "Come look at this. I'll bet we got 25 diamond particles in this sample alone."

Both men quickly moved to the next gravel bar several hundred feet upstream. They took another sample and this time Jerry panned the concentrate. Clay spread out the canvas sheet and climbed under. After several minutes he emerged with a puzzled look on his face.

"Damn," he muttered. "Not a single one. Let's pick another spot."

They looked carefully around and picked another site right on the bedrock of a prominent deposit. Clay took a larger sample this time. Clay removed the concentrate and carefully panned it himself. They both crawled under the canvas.

"How can this be?" Clay said when they again found nothing. "How can we get such good results at the first gravel bar, and such rotten results just a few hundred feet upstream? What's different?" The answer dawned on both at the same moment.

"Christ," muttered Clay, "Those diamond fragments are coming down Montezuma Creek."

They quickly moved the rocker down to the nearly dry bed of Montezuma Creek near a pool of standing water. Clay selected a deposit and shoveled about three cubic feet of gravel into two large canvas bags and dragged them over to the rocker. They quickly washed the sample and scraped the concentrate into a pan. Clay panned the concentrate down to about a half cupful and they nervously placed it under the lamp.

"We've hit it!" Clay exclaimed as they emerged. "Somewhere up Montezuma Creek is the source of our diamonds."

Moving up the canyon, Clay was the first to notice the spongy, undulating surface of a seemingly firm sand bar. It felt like walking on a big air mattress. Clay immediately sprang around, backtracking and calling to Jerry "Go Back! Go Back!"

Jerry stopped dead in his tracks, and began to sink. Jerry realized his predicament and carefully extracted himself and headed for a rock ledge. As long as he kept moving, he couldn't sink. Clay then moved into the streambed, bouncing a little as he proceeded. Great ripples moved gently before him, indicating the unstable nature of the dreaded quicksand deposits found in so many canyon streambeds in southern Utah.

Both Clay and Jerry were aware how treacherous a benign looking sandbar could be, especially when hemmed in by smooth canyon walls, with nothing to grab for or cling to. Once a person sank in over his knees, nothing could prevent him being pulled all the way under. Struggling only made it happen faster. Such quicksand deposits were quite deep, generally over a man's head.

Clay and Jerry could detour around the quicksand, now that it was recognized. However, in a narrow slot canyon, hemmed in by smooth sandstone walls with nowhere to go, the only solution would be to lie down on your back to present the largest possible footprint and wriggle along in a clumsy backstroke, hoping you wouldn't sink. Falling backwards into quicksand was considered a desperate move. But otherwise, unless a companion was nearby to toss you something to pull you out, your fate would be sealed.

Having escaped, Clay and Jerry spent the rest of the day digging samples and all had abundant diamond fragments. But they were all small grains. Clay figured that they must still be some distance from the source.

As Jerry drove them back to Blanding for the evening, Clay studied his geologic map. After a while he turned to Jerry. "This is a real puzzle. Montezuma Creek originates in sedimentary rocks, and diamonds are formed only in a specific type of low silica igneous rocks called peridotites. Where in hell did Montezuma Creek pick up diamonds? There aren't any peridotites anywhere in this region!"

"Maybe Montezuma Creek cuts through an igneous dike somewhere," Jerry said. "It could be an igneous source of peridotite that nobody has discovered. Is that possible?"

"I doubt it," Clay replied. "This area has been thoroughly prospected for uranium, even for coal beds, and it has been thoroughly mapped by government geology crews. How could all those people miss something like an intrusive igneous dike of peridotite? It just doesn't make any sense."

"You know, some coal beds contain pure carbon," Jerry said. "Diamonds are crystalized pure carbon. Maybe there is a connection. Maybe those coal beds you mentioned are the source. What do you think?"

"Not according to what I learned in college," Clay said. "I suggest that we start taking samples farther upstream tomorrow, maybe at Hatch Trading Post. That's where Mr. George says he purchased the pawn jewelry. Maybe there is a connection."

As they turned into the hotel parking area Clay noticed that Lonnie's truck was gone. He went to the office and asked Mrs. Gibbs if anyone had asked for them.

"Why, yes," she answered, "A man did ask just as you drove away. I told him, just like you told me, and he left."

"Do you know if he is coming back tonight?" Clay asked, smiling to himself.

"Oh, no, he checked out and said something about having to make a long dusty ride to Hite Crossing," she said. "How did you boys get back so quick?"

Clay explained that he and Mr. Brooks had just had a change of plans.

The next day they headed to Hatch Trading Post, scouted around and took a few samples. They found a wooded stretch where there was flowing water and quickly washed what they had found. Each sample yielded more fragments. They were still on the right track.

At noon they drove over to the trading post. A small wiry man in his fifties was behind the counter speaking Navajo to three Indians who were making a purchase. Clay recognized the high pitched sing-song tone of the language even though he didn't understand or speak Navajo himself. He remembered that many reservation Indians spoke only Navajo.

As the Indians left, the man at the counter turned to Clay. "Can I be of assistance to you?"

Clay asked if there was anywhere they could get lunch.

"Well, we got cold pop, bread and some sliced meat for sandwiches, but nothing cooked, if that's what you're looking for," he replied. "You men with the oil company?"

"No" Clay replied, surprised. "What oil company? Are there oil companies working around here?"

The man looked at them for a moment with a puzzled expression, then explained that several oil companies, specifically Texaco and Superior Oil, had crews crawling all over the Aneth area immediately east of the trading post drilling oil wells, laying pipelines, building roads, and generally causing an upheaval on the northern Aneth extension of the reservation. He seemed genuinely surprised that Clay and Jerry were unaware of this. It did sound like something that they should have known, until they found out that everyone involved in the oil field development came and went from Durango in southwestern Colorado and Farmington in northwestern New Mexico. As a result San Juan County and Utah were being excluded from the action. That explains the dead-end state highway we drove on yesterday, Clay thought to himself.

Clay then introduced himself and Jerry, and the man at the counter introduced himself as Jed Hatch, a third generation Indian trader at the family-owned Hatch Trading Post.

"I always thought Hatch was a good Mormon name," Jerry said.

"It is, and we are," Jed replied. "Are you men LDS?" Jerry nodded, and Clay shook his head. Jed turned to Jerry. "What brings you down to the reservation?"

Jerry explained that he and Clay were geologists looking for minerals, without being more specific. Jed asked if that included uranium, and Jerry said no. Jed seemed satisfied and turned to show them what he had in the way of lunch fixin's, as he phrased it.

They put together two huge sandwiches on the spot, went outside to a flagstone paved patio at the entrance of the store and sat on a long bench, leaning against the wall of the ancient looking stone building. Jed stood in the doorway talking to them while he waited for his next customer.

"How old is this building?" Clay asked, motioning toward the low stone structure nestled in a grove of immense cottonwood trees.

"My grandpa built the first building in 1904," Jed replied. "At that time this wasn't officially part of the reservation, but there were plenty of Navajos around, and this trading post attracted even more. Navajos are famous for wandering outside the government reservation, herding their sheep, goats and horses wherever there is good grazing to be found. In the old days they went on raids all the way up to Price and over east into the Southern Ute lands in southwestern Colorado." Jed paused. "I suppose you men have heard about the famous Navajo horse trial up in Salt Lake City?"

"Why, No. What trial was that?" Jerry replied.

Jed then old them how the federal government agency in charge of managing the public domain lands on McCracken Mesa got fed up with the Navajos trespassing onto non-Indian lands without a proper grazing lease. "The local boss of the BLM, the government agency, had all the Indian horses rounded up and penned in a big corral," Jed said. "He told the Navajos to come and get 'em, but to be prepared to pay the BLM for the trespass and the forage they had eaten. The Navajos never showed, and the feed bill was getting to be immense, so the BLM boss gave them a final ultimatum, and then ordered the horses slaughtered. The Navajos were outraged, and they hired a lawyer in Salt Lake to sue for damages. Old Judge Willis Ritter, the federal judge in Salt Lake City, got the case. It was well known that Judge Ritter hated the BLM and it turned out he liked the Navajos. His hobby was collecting Navajo rugs. So he ruled that the BLM roundup was illegal and ordered the BLM to pay nearly $2,000 for each horse that they killed. The BLM went crazy! At that price, why every one of those mangy horses would have had to be purebred stock, which of course they weren't. But the price stuck, and eventually the BLM paid!"

"What a story," Clay said, smiling.

"To rub salt into the wound," Jed concluded, "Somebody in Congress got wind of the story, and introduced legislation to officially add McCracken

Mesa to the Navajo Indian Reservation. If it becomes law, pretty soon the Navajos will own all the lands they got accused of trespassing on. That BLM boss almost got himself fired and I'll bet he wishes he'd never got involved with those Navajo horses in the first place."

"Where is this McCracken Mesa?" Clay asked, laughing.

"Why, all this land around here, and that big mesa you drove across to get here, that's McCracken Mesa," explained Jed, waving his arms north and west.

Clay stopped laughing. Holy Cow, he thought to himself, this guy's telling us our prime prospecting area might become Indian lands in the near future.

After lunch, back in the Jeep, Clay turned to Jerry. "We've got a serious problem. If this Montezuma Creek area is about to become part of the reservation, it will be closed to prospecting. We've got to find the source of the diamonds fast, while there is still a chance for us to stake mining claims. Those Navajos have a reputation for being impossible to deal with when it comes to exploring for mineral deposits. The uranium prospectors and the AEC got a cold reception when they approached the tribe, and there are damn few uranium mines within the reservation as a result. We don't want to fall into that trap!"

Jerry agreed, and they determined to speed up their efforts, deciding to set up a field camp near the trading post to avoid the long drive from Blanding every day. Going back inside, Clay and Jerry asked Jed about a place. Jed offered to rent them a shady spot down by the creek next to running water. They could get drinking water from the post well. They happily accepted his offer and left for Blanding to purchase supplies before the big grocery store there closed for the day.

On the way in, Jerry suggested that he should be the camp cook, and pick out the food supplies. Clay was surprised, but was secretly relieved. Before long they pulled up to Parley Redd Merchantile, a large rambling stone building that seemed to sell everything, groceries, kitchen items, clothing and some hardware items. Jerry avoided canned goods, pointing out that the trading post carried block ice for refrigeration. He insisted that they invest in a large portable ice chest.

Jerry had been spoiled by the good cooking down on the river, and he wanted to get away from Clay's canned food and dried beans. Instead, Jerry bought fresh meats, fruit and vegetables. As he explained, he didn't want to have to drive into town to eat a decent meal.

After shopping, they stopped by Charlie Nevilles' place to see if Nancy had heard anything from her husband, and if she knew when he might be back. She hadn't but said that Charlie's hired helper, the van driver, was going to meet the party at Crossing of the Fathers on the Colorado River next Friday. He was scheduled to leave the next day to make the two day drive.

Clay then asked if Charlie had an extra tent they could rent, for a few weeks or so.

"Oh, I know he has lots of extra camp equipment. Why don't you fellows take this key to the equipment shed and see what you might need. You can settle on a price after he returns," she replied, handing Clay a ring of keys.

Clay and Jerry poked around and soon found a large wall tent, a cook fly, two folding canvas cots, a gasoline camping stove, lanterns and everything they could possibly need. Jerry even discovered a medium sized dutch oven. Clay made a list of the equipment and handed it to Nancy back in the house.

"My, you fellows sure plan on setting up a comfortable camp," she said. "Sure you can get it all into that Jeep? You must not plan to move, once you get your camp set up." Jerry laughed and explained that he wasn't a sleep-on-the-ground camper, like Clay. He liked his creature comforts.

They stuffed all the camping gear into the cavernous maw of the boxy Jeep station wagon, and were barely able to close the rear gate. Clay was relieved to see that it all fit because he had dreaded driving the long dusty road back to Hatch Trading Post with the rear of the station wagon gaping open, sucking in all the road dust. With the rocker tied on top, they looked like a gypsy caravan on the move.

They planned spending a last night in the King Hotel, taking long hot showers, probably their last for many days. They then headed for the Town Cafe, early as usual.

"Where you boys been?" Janie said as they came in. "I figured you must have gone to Salt Lake, or back down on the river. Some grubby looking guys were asking about you."

"Did they say who they were?"

"They didn't say, but I think they were uranium miners. Least they looked like miners. One of them I've seen before, and he was the one doing all the asking. I told them you were geologists from Salt Lake City, and that you had been down on the San Juan River looking for minerals. The one man, he asked where

Piute Farms was, and I told him it was down on the river. Soon after that they left."

"Well, we're on our way back down to the San Juan River, somewhere downstream from Mexican Hat," Clay said, smiling over at Jerry. "Just in case anybody's interested."

Most of the following morning was spent setting up their camp and settling in. Several Navajo men and boys came over to get a look. Clay and Jerry had difficulty communicating without Jed being there. Neither had been around reservation Navajos before, most of whom wore a distinctive costume and lived a lifestyle that seemed alien to most white folks.

Since the 1600s, when Spanish settlers entered the region and first introduced Navajos to domestic sheep, the principle livelihood of the Navajos had been sheep herding and weaving elaborately patterned wool rugs for sale or trade. Only much later did a few Navajos learn silversmithing, also from the Spanish. Living as they do in a barren desert, the Navajos have to range over large areas to find forage for their herds. Being very inventive, the sheepherders learned to trick the not-so-smart sheep into foraging steep slopes and high ledges by introducing goats into the sheep herds. The more adventuresome goats, being natural climbers, could reach any greenery in the rough terrain and the sheep simply follow them. The Navajo women share herding duties with the men, but women are the sole weavers of the world famous Navajo rugs. It is generally supposed that some of the intricate patterns are based on similar intricate sand paintings done by Navajo men in ritual ceremonies, then destroyed at the conclusion of each ceremony.

All the older Navajo women around Hatch Trading Post wore dark velveteen blouses and long velveteen or heavy satin skirts, and were decked out in all the massive silver and turquoise jewelry they could afford. In fact, it is said that a Navajo woman wears her entire wealth in the form of silver jewelry. The local Navajo men, on the other hand, wear ordinary western clothes and little jewelry, except sometimes fancy bolo ties and silver belt buckles on dress-up occasions. Most Navajo men wear massive wide western tooled leather belts and large black wide brimmed felt hats, although a few wear colorful bandannas wrapped around their heads. Cowboy boots and work boots were common on the men, but the women all wear high soft leather moccasins. Women's skirts are often fringed with silver buttons, or sometimes silver bells. Young children wear clothes similar to the adults, but without ornamentation or jewelry. Teenagers are seldom seen at Hatch Trading Post. Jed explained that most school-aged children are sent away for schooling, most to far off boarding schools run by the U.S. Bureau of Indian Affairs.

After lunch at their tent camp, Clay headed up to the trading post while Jerry puttered around with the cooking gear.

"Tell me exactly where this McCracken Mesa area lies with respect to Montezuma Canyon," Clay asked Jed, unrolling his maps.

Jed took a look and pointed out what he knew. The north boundary was about five miles up Montezuma Creek above the trading post, he said, and ran about 12 miles due west all the way to Recapture Creek, taking in an immense area north of the San Juan River. Jed remarked that two BLM employees visited this area frequently, inspecting for mining claims, and could identify the boundaries of the extension.

"The BLM is inspecting mining claims?" Clay asked. "Who has mining claims down here?"

"The whole area is plastered with uranium claims," Jed replied. "Bud Menlove and Jack Glover operate a small mine up Montezuma Creek, and between them and all the other prospectors that roam this area, I doubt if there is any unclaimed ground in this part of the county. There are uranium shows 'most everywhere that the Morrison formation beds are exposed, you know. Would you like to meet Menlove next time he comes through?"

"Yeah, I'd like to talk to him," Clay said, "But we're prospecting for gravel beds, not uranium."

"What in the world do you expect to find in gravel beds, especially 'way out here?" Jed asked in surprise.

Caught off guard, Clay did some fast thinking. "Jerry runs a rock shop up in Salt Lake, and I'm helping him find specimens he can sell to tourists. Petrified wood, things like that," he said.

"Oh, that," said Jed. "Well, the Morrison formation is filled with petrified logs and dinosaur bones. We sometimes get rock collectors from Colorado and California looking for petrified wood and fossil dinosaur bones. There must be quite a market for things like that. There are some petrified river channel deposits in the Morrison formation that carry enormous petrified logs and big pieces of dinosaur bone. There's a dandy deposit up in Alkali Wash, just above this post that has attracted lots of rock collectors lately. But no uranium. You know, petrified logs and uranium are generally found together in the uranium mines all around these parts. Uranium prospectors routinely look for petrified logs in their search for uranium, but these logs around here don't contain any uranium. But they sure are pretty petrified logs, brightly colored red and yellow and purple, and some jet black with thin white cracks. Here, look at these pieces," he said, digging behind his counter and pulling out several agatized specimens. "There are some larger petrified logs lining the walk just outside the entrance door to this building," he added.

As Clay slowly walked back to camp, he thought about what Jed had said. Could gravel deposits deposited over a hundred million years ago be the source of the large diamonds they were looking for?

He shared his thoughts with Jerry. "Well, if diamonds occur in petrified river gravel deposits, our trusty gold rocker should be able to find them," Jerry said. "If not, well, we'll just have to keep on looking. Petrified river gravels are just rivers of stone, instead of rivers with water. That doesn't sound any more far-fetched than the idea of undiscovered peridotite intrusions in this sedimentary region."

That afternoon Clay and Jerry drove slowly up the much traveled rut road in the dry bed of Montezuma Canyon, inspecting the sandstone and mud-stone canyon walls closely. They noticed several exposures of fossilized stream channels in the Morrison formation. Where the creek erosion had cut across these fossil stream channels composed of silicified gravel deposits, truly a river of stone, Clay thought, the soft sediments on either side of the fossil stream bed had been eroded away, leaving the erosion-resistant petrified channel as a low transverse ridge lying at an angle to the modern canyon and the creek bed at its bottom. These fossil river channels now resembled low ridges cutting across the floor of the canyon, at least for the short distances between the modern canyon walls. It would make for interesting prospecting.

Wherever they spotted gravel deposits at or near bedrock in the bottoms of the fossilized stream channels, Clay took three cubic foot samples at each site. He took similar sized samples at sites in the bed of the modern creek channel itself. Because the creek bed was completely dry in this part of the canyon, they had to put all their samples into large canvas bag to take back to camp, where the rocker could be set up next to the stream.

They took a total of five samples, two from different fossil channel exposures, and three from the loose gravels in the modern creek bed which Clay carefully identified with paper tags. The last sample was taken about five miles up Montezuma Canyon from the trading post, at about the place Jed had pointed out as the northern boundary of the McCracken Mesa Extension.

Back at camp, while Jerry busied himself cooking diner, Clay set the rocker up by the creek and dragged the samples down so it would be ready to go after dinner.

They were just getting ready to eat when two men dressed in khakis walked up, and introduced themselves as Bud Menlove and Jack Glover. They said Jed Hatch had suggested they speak to them, something about prospecting for petrified wood.

"That's right," Clay said. "I'm Clay Greer and this is Jerry Brooks who owns Jerry's Lapidary and Supplies, a rock shop in Salt Lake."

"I know your rock shop well," Menlove said, looking at Jerry, "It's where I buy my prospecting supplies. I live just north of Salt Lake, in Bountiful." Turning to Clay, he asked, "Don't I know you? Your name is mighty familiar, but I don't recognize your face."

"I can't imagine where you might have heard my name," Clay stammered. "Maybe it's someone else named Greer," he said lamely.

Menlove and Glover then said they had a small operating uranium mine about ten miles up Montezuma Creek, and they held numerous mining claims in the vicinity. It soon became clear that these mining claims fell right in the middle of the prime prospecting area Clay and Jerry had recently identified. Clay did some fast thinking.

"Since we're not interested in uranium deposits, do you think we can work out an arrangement to prospect your claims for the stuff we're interested in? We would call your attention to any uranium signs we run across," Clay said. "We might be willing to pay you a reasonable royalty for any petrified wood, or bones, or anything else we extract from your claims that isn't connected to uranium deposits." He held his breath.

"What kind of a royalty?" Menlove asked Clay.

"Ten cents a pound!" Jerry interjected. "That's what I customarily pay for raw material, regardless of what I'm able to sell the material for in my shop. That way, you get your money and you don't have to follow every sale, and we don't get into endless arguments." Jerry spoke with such authority that his proposal was promptly accepted.

"I'll put something in writing for all of us to sign," Jerry said, taking charge.

As they shook hands, Menlove told Jerry to drive up to their mine late tomorrow with his papers. They would leave the details up to him, which suited Jerry fine.

"Geez," Clay exclaimed as their visitors drove away, "You drive a mighty businesslike bargain, Mr. Brooks. I'm very impressed and I'm glad you jumped in. Ten cents a pound, is that what you pay for rock shop inventory?"

"You bet, that's my standard rate," Jerry said, smiling, "I turn around and sell the material for 50 to 75 cents a pound. I consider that a very good price for alluvial diamonds, don't you?"

"First we've got to find the diamonds," Clay said, "But let's eat so we'll have time to test our samples."

By the time they finished it was getting dark, so Clay suggested they wash their samples by the light of one of their gasoline lanterns. Working fast in the growing cold, they quickly concentrated the five samples and Clay laid out the concentrates in separate aluminum pie tins, in exactly the order they had been taken originally, while Jerry set up the ultraviolet lamp.

"Holy B'Geezus!" exclaimed Jerry as he waived the lamp over the pie tins. The concentrates fairly bristled with bright blue fluorescent specks, a few as big as rice grains. Two of the pans contained more and larger diamond particles than the others, while one pan contained only a few specks. "We have a definite trend here," Jerry said. "What do your notes tell us, Clay?"

"It tells us we've got the answer to our riddle, I think," Clay replied. Thumbing carefully through his pad and the labels, Clay continued, "Both of the rich samples came from the fossil gravel deposits and the weakest one came from the creek bed farthest up Montezuma Creek. I think this indicates we're running out of the deposit as we continue up the canyon. Clearly, the source of our diamonds is the fossil channels, if my stratigraphy is correct." He paused. "Jerry, your so-called Rivers of Stone have turned out to be the key."

"By Golly, these diamonds must have been deposited at the same time that dinosaurs roamed this region," Jerry said. "Man, can you imagine conditions during the Jurassic Age, 160 million years ago, when this region was jungles and mountains? Big floods must have created streambeds filled with dinosaur carcasses, fallen trees and, now diamond deposits. This is an incredible discovery, Clay."

Clay nodded, carefully plucking out the grain sized diamonds, fourteen in all, and placed them in a glass vial, which he labeled. He then washed each concentrate into its own vial and labeled them.

"Tomorrow we'll try to identify the richest of the fossil stream channels," Clay said. "Old Jed said something about a dandy fossil channel he saw over in Alkali Wash. We ought to check that out, too."

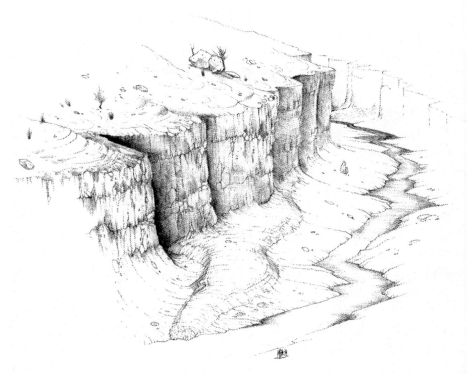

"River of Stone" outcroping in a canyon.

108

9

ALKALI WASH

The next morning Clay asked Jed Hatch if he had any writing paper, carbon paper, and perhaps a typewriter. Jed had all three and offered Clay the use of his cluttered desk in an equally cluttered back room. After more than an hour, and four drafts later, he had accomplished his mission and headed back to camp.

"How does this fit the bill," Clay said, handing a one and one-half page document to Jerry. "I kept it as short as I could but I don't think I left anything out. What do you think?"

"It looks okay to me," replied Jerry after reading it twice. "I think it's slick how you slipped in the precious and semi-precious reference. At first glance it seems to refer to agatized material, but it actually refers to everything we extract from the deposit. Good thinking."

Clay proposed that they spend the day exploring the area and mapping all of the fossil stream channels they can find, rather than sampling. Sampling was hard work, so Jerry readily agreed. Both were anxious to look around, now that they felt they had found the source of the diamonds.

Taking everything out of the Jeep but necessary gear, they set out for Montezuma Canyon and its tributaries, particularly Alkali Wash. During the morning they inspected six fossil channels that would warrant further exploration and sampling, but the most interesting by far was the one in Alkali Wash, just as Jed Hatch had said.

In Jurassic times, 160 million years ago, numerous fast flowing streams deposited coarse gravels in meandering channels in a muddy delta area, probably the flood detritus from nearby igneous mountain uplifts. Those mountains must have been made of ultramafic rocks, because diamonds occur only in high temperature molten rocks containing high magnesium-aluminum-iron constituents and exceptionally low silica.

The classic host rock for diamonds in South Africa is Kimberlite and that rock is just one of a family of rocks known generically as peridotites. True Kimberlites were known to occur only in South Africa, while diamonds have been discovered and produced in India, Brazil and British Guinea. Surprisingly, most commercial diamond deposits are alluvial accumulations, and many are alluvial reworkings of fossil alluvial deposits, where the original primary source of the diamonds is still unknown. Diamonds are so hard they resist wearing down as the alluvial deposits are washed around, being deposited and redeposited many times.

The local fossil stream channels were eventually buried in mud, after which they became further compacted by the weight of successive sedimentary formations, and cemented by percolating ground water carrying silica in solution. Apparently these particular stream channels also carried trees and animal carcasses out onto the primeval mud flats where they, too, were buried by mud and subjected to the action of silica-bearing ground water. It is the chemical nature of things for organic material, wood and bones, to be gradually replaced, cell by cell, by silica dropping out of solution in ground water. That is how virtually all plant and animal fossils are turned into stone and thus preserved. The microscopic details preserved by this slow replacement of organic cells by amorphous silica, which can ultimately harden into agate, are remarkable.

Much later the compacted mud beds, called shale, siltstone and mudstone, became uplifted and through stream and wind erosion over incredible time spans eventually were re-exposed at the surface. For every existing surface exposure of a geologic deposit, there is generally much more still beneath the surface awaiting eventual exposure, and probably even more that has already been eroded away and lost. The term erosional remnant refers to an exposure at the surface where virtually all the geologic bed has already eroded away and lost.

In the case of the large fossil stream channel in Alkali Wash, the softer enclosing mudstone had been quite eroded, exposing the harder channel deposit as a conspicuous low ridge of silicified stream gravel laced with petrified logs, large scattered dinosaur bones and other detrital materials generally found in flashflood outwashes. At Alkali Wash the enclosing mudstone had even been washed away from beneath the edges of the fossil stream channel, allowing an observer to walk up under the fossil channel and view portions of its bottom.

Clay and Jerry were awestruck as they inspected the bottom of a river bed that had been deposited 160 million years ago, and saw the jackstraw piles of petrified trees and entangled dinosaur carcasses and large bones just as they had accumulated so long ago.

In the canyon wall on the opposite side the fossil stream channel disappeared beneath hundreds of feet of overlying beds, but it was obvious that by tunneling along the route of the channel one could follow it for great distances in either direction. In fact, Clay thought he might be able to trace one channel from its exposure in Montezuma Canyon to another weak exposure in a tributary canyon, but he couldn't be sure.

Clay and Jerry inspected and mapped all the other fossil channels they could find. Late in the afternoon Clay suggested that they drive to the uranium mine up Montezuma Creek before it got too late. Jerry reluctantly agreed and they headed out.

On the drive up it seemed that the strata containing the fossil channels inclined gently downward, while the floor of the canyon gradually climbed. Any fossil channels were buried in strata beneath the canyon floor, Clay thought. Soon they spotted mine dumps on the east flank of the canyon and a dirt road turning off to the east up a tributary canyon toward a small cluster of shacks and equipment.

"We've been expecting you fellows," Bud Menlove called out to them as they got out of the Jeep. Jack Glover and two other men in dirty overalls were standing nearby. "Come on in," Jack said.

Inside the dark shack there was a strong smell of diesel fuel and lubricating oil. Greasy machine parts were lying all around and Clay saw a large sheet of plywood on a cluster of 55-gallon drums which served as a table. There were no chairs.

Jerry pulled out a large envelope and handed it to Menlove. "Here," Jerry said. "Read this and see if it does what we agreed to yesterday."

Bud read the papers slowly with Jack looking over his shoulder.

"It looks okay to me," Bud said, turning to his partner, "How do you like it, Jack?" Jack nodded. "Where's this ten dollars you say we're getting at signing? We can use every penny." Bud laughed, handing the papers back to Jerry.

"As soon as you sign I'll be glad to pay you," Clay said, reaching for his wallet.

"There's two copies there," Jerry said, "We get one signed copy, and you get the other. Plus the ten dollars."

"Well, let's do it," Menlove responded, reaching for his ballpoint pen. Bud signed both copies first, then Jack, and finally Jerry and Clay. Clay then placed a ten dollar bill on the carbon copy and handed it to Bud.

"Now that we are business associates," Clay said, "can we see a map of your claims so we'll know when we're on your ground?"

"We got a map," Bud replied, "but only one copy. You're welcome to look at it and make notes," he said, taking a glued-together montage of USGS topographic maps down off the rough plank wall and laying it out on the table.

"No problem," Clay said. "Let me go out to the Jeep and get my maps. I can transfer your claim information right onto them."

As Clay traced the claim boundaries onto his maps, he noticed that their uranium claims pretty well blanketed the area he and Jerry had been exploring that morning. He saw few open areas not held by the Menlove/Glover claims, called the "Yellow Bird Group".

"Whose claims are these, farther up Alkali Wash?" Clay asked Bud, pointing to another claim group. He couldn't read the smudged notes identifying those claims.

Bud looked at his smudged notes. "Oh, those are phony claims owned by some crook up in Salt Lake named Arcarus or something. He files phony affidavits of annual assessment labor every year, and you can't find his claim monuments, except for a few down by the road. His claims are called the Emperor Group, but they're completely phony."

Clay's heart missed a beat, and he turned to face Menlove, "Could that claim owner be John S. Arcarius, the land broker and promoter?"

"Yeah, that's his name. That's him. Do you know him?" Bud asked.

Clay confirmed Bud's evaluation of the man and his methods, but made it plain that he didn't count Arcarius among his friends or associates. Bud seemed relieved, and Clay sensed that the two men were competitors, if not downright enemies.

"When you guys gonna start taking petrified wood out so's we can start receiving our royalty?" Jack asked, smiling.

Jerry explained that they wouldn't be removing anything for a while. He then said he would put in a scale to weigh each load and pointed out that the agreement required him to give them monthly reports and send them a check for what he took. "If you gentlemen want to put in your own scales, or station someone at the operation to watch what is taken out, that can be arranged," he said.

Bud said they'd check the operation from time to time, but Jerry's arrangements were satisfactory for now. They shook hands and Clay and Jerry climbed into the Jeep and headed for camp.

"That went smoothly," Jerry remarked, as they drove down Montezuma Creek. When Clay told Jerry who John S. Arcarius was, and his hostile relationship with him, Jerry was silent for a while. "I sure hope we don't have to deal with a guy like that," he said finally. "These two fellows seem like straight arrows, interested in making a few bucks. That promoter in Salt Lake sounds like a weasel."

It was getting dark as they approached the mouth of Alkali Wash. Jerry turned to Clay. "Let's stop by the fossil deposit before we go back to camp. I brought along the ultraviolet lamps, and I'd like to look at the bottom of that channel in the dark. You game?"

"Sure," Clay replied, and turned up the wash. He got as close as he could, and walked the rest of the way until they stood directly under the channel. Jerry switched on the long wave lamp and directed it upward.

"My God," Clay gasped, as petrified logs and other detritus glowed different colors in the pale violet beam.

"Ain't that beautiful?" Jerry said. "I knew from specimens in my shop that agatized and opalized wood will fluoresce bright colors, but seeing it in nature is really something."

"Let me see that short wave lamp," Clay said. Placing the lens right next to the bottom of the deposit, Clay moved slowly along, stopping from time to time, then moving on.

"Christ, come look at this, Jerry!" Clay shouted. "It's a pocket of diamonds and one of them is a big one!"

Jerry quickly pulled out his pocket knife and in a few minutes Clay filled his shirt pocket with material. Further searching revealed no more pockets in the area, but Clay was ecstatic about their discovery.

Back in camp over a dinner hotly prepared by Jerry, they planned their operations. For the time being, they intended to do a detailed inspection, in daylight and dark, of each fossil channel. Some excavation would be required to dig away the soft shale around the deposits, and chop away at the cemented gravels to get at any diamonds. Somehow they needed to get water to the deposit so they wouldn't have to haul everything down to the creek to wash it in the rocker. Jerry reminded Clay that they also needed to mine petrified wood and dinosaur bone so any observers wouldn't become suspicious. This would involve some serious mining, and that would require strong backs, tools and equipment. Jerry insisted that any wood or bone they removed and paid for was going back to his shop in Salt Lake City, and that would require some transportation.

By the light of the gasoline lantern Jerry worked out a new budget for the mining operation he envisioned, detailing manpower and equipment requirements, and estimated expenses. It was a sobering exercise trying to divvy up the new costs. Jerry offered to finance half, if Clay would shoulder the other half. That way they would be 50-50 partners for all the petrified wood and dinosaur bone they recovered. Mr. George and his partners would own all diamonds recovered. Mining for wood and bone would give them a cover to prospect for buried diamonds. The value of the diamonds might exceed the value of the wood and bone recovered, but while they were assured of recovering valuable wood and bone, diamond recovery wasn't a sure thing. Jerry was convinced that the fossil wood and bone operation would be a profitable venture, but how to split the costs was the problem. Everything was contingent on Mr. George's approval of Jerry's new budget; he was the boss, after all.

Of all the channels explored the rest of the week, only three lent themselves to easy exploitation. The Alkali Wash deposit remained their best bet, so they decided to concentrate their efforts there. Jerry took charge of all onsite operations, and scoped out a plan of development and mining that focused on recovery of petrified wood and dinosaur bone. Clay worked with the gravels and processed them for diamonds.

Jerry then asked Jed Hatch if any of the local Navajos could be hired to do the heavy labor. Jed turned out to be a gold mine of information and assistance. He recommended individual Navajos, and told Jerry where he could purchase or rent equipment from idle or distressed uranium mines in the vicinity. He particularly recommended Peter Shonto who had worked as a uranium miner and who spoke both English and Navajo. "He'll make a perfect boss," Jed said.

Jed volunteered to be Jerry's unpaid employment agent and set up job interviews. Jerry said he needed three men immediately, perhaps a few more later.

Back at the camp, Jerry told Clay what he had arranged and they decided that one of them should go to Salt Lake for materials and meet with Mr. George and work out a revised agreement. Jerry offered his pickup truck to haul supplies down to their operation.

Jerry needed to stay at Hatch to interview laborers and arrange for equipment, so Clay would make the trip. Jerry would need the Jeep, so they decided he would drive Clay to Monticello where he could catch a Trailways bus to Salt Lake. But first they would have to drive to Blanding to settle up with Charlie Nevilles and to telephone Mr. George in Los Angeles to arrange for a meeting with Clay in Salt Lake.

"What am I supposed to tell Mary?" Clay said.

"Just tell her I'm too busy setting up an operation that will put us on easy street for the rest of our lives," Jerry replied, laughing. "She'll understand."

Clay then packed a duffle bag with clothes and the diamonds and they headed for Blanding. Charlie Nevilles wasn't back yet, so Clay put in his call to Los Angeles to arrange a meeting, and they drove on to Monticello. Jerry waited around until the bus arrived and then headed back. It would be nearly a week before they saw each other again.

Clay telephoned Mary Brooks when he arrived in Salt Lake. It was early morning and the all-night bus ride left Clay exhausted. He explained their plans to Mary and she offered to pick Clay up while her oldest daughter drove Mary's car to the rock shop. Clay could just drop her off at the shop.

When they got to the shop Clay and Mary packed the supplies detailed on Jerry's list into cardboard boxes. It would take a few days to get everything coordinated, so Clay stored everything at the shop until he was ready to leave.

Two days later Mr. George arrived and Clay met him at the Newhouse Hotel for dinner. Clay showed him the diamonds and samples, demonstrating how they fluoresced bright blue under the shortwave ultraviolet lamp. He even drew a diagram and a sketch map of the fossil stream channels, and explained how he and Jerry were planning to mine petrified wood and dinosaur bone as a cover while they continued prospecting for the diamonds. Then he presented Jerry's new budget for the combined operations.

"Mr. Greer, you seem to have solved the geological mystery, but you have yet to find a valuable deposit of the gemstones. Am I correct?"

"Well, yes, that's correct," Clay stammered. "But we first had to find where the diamonds were coming from."

"Mr. Greer," he continued in a strangely formal tone, "I and my partners are businessmen, and not scientists. You have solved the scientific puzzle, but we are not yet close to a commercial success. Wouldn't you agree?"

"Yes," Clay responded, his heart sinking.

"I think Mr. Brooks' proposal has merit, but I wish to limit the time and cap the expenses in a way that will protect my investors. Let's make an arrangement for another 30 days. Then we should be able to better decide what to do. Is that agreeable?"

"As a strictly temporary arrangement, I think we can accept that," Clay said. "You've been fair with us, and we have been the same with you." Clay sat back, hoping Jerry would concur.

"Good, I'll make some interlineations on Mr. Brooks' budget proposal here and we can sign it. I understand that the hotel has some sort of a machine to make a copy for you."

After dinner they said goodnight and Clay went over to his office across the street. He had been surprised by Mr. George's restrained response to his exciting news, and he needed to think.

Clay finally decided he had done all he had come to do, so he planned an early start in the morning. He telephoned Mary at home that evening. Just after sun up, he met Mary and loaded the supplies into the pickup. He could do his real thinking on the road.

Willys Jeep station wagon on the road to Elk Ridge.

116

10

THE FOSSIL MINE

It was well after dark by the time Clay reached Blanding, so he decided to spend the night at the King Hotel rather than drive into their camp so late.

Clay checked in and then headed to the Town Cafe for dinner. As he walked in Janie looked up, surprised.

"Well, I had about given you boys up as customers," she said. "Where have you boys been?"

"I've been up in Salt Lake, and Jerry's been down south, doing his own meals. I've sure missed your home cooking."

Janie smiled and handed him a menu. "You remember those miners who were asking about you?" she said. "One of them was through here just yesterday, asking about you fellows again. I told him I hadn't seen either of you in nearly two weeks, and assumed you guys had left the country."

"Did he say where he was headed?" Clay asked.

Janie thought a minute. "No, but he said something about visiting your camp at Piute Farms, but you weren't there. He did mention they ran out of food and ate all the supplies you had left there. He seemed awfully disappointed you didn't return."

Clay ordered the special, baked meat loaf, and thanked Janie for being such a good friend. He wondered where the Baker brothers had gone. After finishing dinner he drove back to the hotel, looking around for their truck, but it couldn't be seen.

Early the next morning Clay was up and on the road, and he got to camp as Jerry was just cooking breakfast. "Can I interest you in some flapjacks and eggs?" Jerry said, smiling. "Boy, am I glad to see you! I've got lots of things to tell you, and I think you'll be pleased at our progress. How did your meeting with Mr. George go?"

"He didn't react quite like I thought he would, but he liked your proposal and we signed a new agreement. It's only good for a month, but it's essentially the one you made up." Digging into his duffle bag, he pulled out an envelope and handed it to Jerry. "Read this, then give me your reaction."

"Well, he didn't make any changes I find objectionable. I was afraid he would want a piece of our fossil business."

"No, he definitely doesn't want any part of that," Clay said. "In fact, he was concerned that we would saddle his investors with the expenses of our operations."

"I tell you, Clay," Jerry said, "This fossil operation is a guaranteed money maker. I can sell that stuff at a tremendous profit. Unless we find an awful lot of diamonds, and big ones at that, it is fossil wood and bone that will make us some real money."

"Well, we've got 30 days to find a commercial accumulation of diamonds, or Mr. George and his mysterious investor group may pull the plug, so I'm glad you're so optimistic."

Jerry then told Clay how he had hired Pete Shonto and two other Navajos, rented an air compressor and a pneumatic mining loader, erected his mail order screens, and installed a large galvanized water trough to supply water onsite for the rocker. He had already started to stockpile beautiful petrified wood and had found some exceptionally high quality agatized dinosaur bone, gem quality he called it.

"I've got a big pile of likely looking gravel for you and the Indians to put through the rocker," Jerry said. "I think we ought to hire two more Navajos to run the rocker, at least until you process all the gravel we've got on hand."

"Let's go up to Alkali Wash this morning," Clay said. "I'd like to see what you've done. Incidentally, I was able to find some more ultraviolet lamps in Salt Lake, so mining in the dark for fluorescent diamonds should be very productive if we can dig away the mudstone to expose the bottom of the channels."

Clay and Jerry then jumped into the Jeep and headed for Alkali Wash. It barely resembled the place Clay had seen only a week before. The three Navajos were shoveling and pushing mudstone from under the gravel bed of the stream channel, using the compressed air loader like a miniature bulldozer. There were neat piles of petrified logs and chunks of agatized material, and Jerry led Clay over to a small mound of bright red and yellow agate, identifying it as gem grade agatized dinosaur bone. The cellular structure of the bone was clearly visible, but each piece was a solid, smooth agate. Clay was impressed. Close by were larger agatized dinosaur bones, shank, knuckle and all.

"These bones have no value at all to paleontologists and scientists, because these are isolated bones and fragments, but lapidarists and jewelry makers will go nuts over this material," Jerry shouted over the roar of the gasoline powered compressor. "I can sell this material, as is, for $15 or more a pound. The lapidarists can slab it and sell it for $50 a pound or more, and polish small pieces into cabochons for jewelry and sell them for at least $10 each. Jewelers and craftsmen can create bolo ties, belt buckles, broaches and pendant earrings and sell them like hotcakes. This is some of the finest agate material I have ever seen. Look at this piece," he said, holding up a piece taken at random from the pile. The colors were brilliant.

Clay then inspected the gravel. Some was still cemented in lumps and would have to be broken up. Jerry's mail order screens would separate out the isolated lumps, which the workers could then break with a sledge hammer. It would be a slow business to wash all of the gravel. Clay decided to check the channel deposits with the lamps after dark. Where he had been able to find one pocket, there ought to be others.

Jerry introduced Clay to his Navajo workers, Pete Shonto, Billy Tsai and Walt Chuska. Billy and Walt spoke very little English, but Pete spoke excellent English and knew quite a lot about mining. He was the work boss. Clay remembered Mr. George's story about the Code Talkers of the South Pacific in World War II. He wondered if any of these men had been in the war.

Next Clay took a look at Jerry's setup for operating the rocker. Jerry had gotten a large corrugated iron watering trough and filled it with about 10 inches of water. The rocker was set up on a plank frame over it, so water could be dipped from the trough into the hopper, and the outflow would empty back into the trough. In this manner the water could be used over and over with very little spillage. When the trough filled up with detrital overflow from the rocker, it could be shoveled out from time to time. It was a primitive method, but it would work for now.

Clay then showed Pete Shonto how to run gravel through the rocker and Pete caught on immediately. After a while this guy could run the whole operation without Jerry and me, Clay thought to himself. He motioned Jerry to a quiet spot away from the compressor . "Do any of these fellows know we're looking for diamonds?"

"Of course not," Jerry replied, "I just told them that we're collecting petrified wood and bone, and that when you came we would also be checking the gravel for whatever it contains."

"How did you find this guy?" Clay asked, pointing to Peter Shonto.

"Jed Hatch first recommended him to me, and steered me to all these men. He told me he can get others when we need them. They are good, hard workers. They like the idea of working near their homes, and being able to go home every night. I tell you, Clay, this is a perfect situation."

Toward sundown Clay and Jerry called it a day and loaded everybody into the Jeep for the ride to Hatch.

After supper back at camp, Clay and Jerry gathered up the ultraviolet lamps and some tools, and headed back to Alkali Wash. In the semi-darkness Clay lamped the underside of the stream channel deposit carefully, particularly in places exposed by the recent digging. Wherever he saw the blue fluorescence he fastened red plastic flagging to mark the spot. However, he didn't find another pocket of diamonds, and he was disappointed. But when he lamped the gravel pile he spotted a single bean-sized diamond and plucked it out, smiling. "Another specimen for Mr. George's collection," he said.

Returning to camp, they panned the rocker concentrate down at the creek by the light of a gasoline lantern. The concentrate contained numerous small flecks of diamonds, but no large grains. Clay was again quietly disappointed.

Next morning, as Jerry was washing up the breakfast dishes, a green Jeep station wagon exactly like Clay's drove up. Two young men in khaki pants and shirts got out. They introduced themselves as Wayne Moore and Hubert Norris, BLM geologists working in the vicinity, inspecting mining claims.

"Jed Hatch tells us you fellows want to know about the McCracken Mesa Extension to the Navajo Indian Reservation, where the boundaries lines were, and how it might affect your operations."

It turned out that all of their work sites were within the area to be added to the reservation and that the BLM had withdrawn the entire area from location of new mining claims under the U.S. Mining Laws in anticipation that the identified lands would eventually pass to the Navajo Nation. The BLM geologists were scouting the area to identify mining claims already located on the lands and determine if those claims were valid. Valid mining claims would be preserved in any land transferred to the Navajos.

"How many mining claims have you already inspected on McCracken Mesa?" Jerry asked.

"Oh, nearly all,"replied Wayne Moore, "We've been at this for nearly a year."

"And how many valid claims have you found," Jerry asked.

"None," said Mr. Moore.

Clay's heart stopped. "Have you inspected the Yellow Bird Group over in Alkali Wash, the ones owned by Bud Menlove and Jack Glover?"

Moore looked at his companion, then at Clay. "We know those claims and none of them within the project boundary are valid. Do you have some special interest in those claims?"

"How can you say the Yellow Bird claims in Alkali Wash are invalid," Jerry blurted out. "What gives you guys the power to say a mining claim is valid or invalid?"

Clay broke in. "Is this decision final?"

Wayne Moore had taken a step back at Jerry's outburst. "Well, no," he said, addressing Clay, "our findings are only recommendations to our superiors. But we've checked out those claims and determined they contain no valuable locatable mineral deposit on the date the lands were withdrawn by the BLM. Those are the official standards for deciding whether a claim is valid or invalid."

"What happens to a mining claim, one that you guys say is invalid, if your recommendations are approved?" Clay said.

Wayne Moore explained the complex process involved to invalidate a claim, saying that there was an opportunity for the claim owner to present evidence at an administrative trial to prove his claim is valid. He also explained the administrative appeals process and bureaucratic steps to insure fair treatment.

Jerry stepped in. "How can you say these claims don't contain a valuable mineral deposit? We've extracted valuable petrified wood and dinosaur bone, all beautifully agatized material."

"Fossils are not locatable minerals under BLM interpretations of the mining law," Norris replied. "Agate, well, that's another matter, but the deadline for finding any deposit to validate a mining claim is over one year ago. When did you discover this agate?"

Clay broke in. "When did you say these mining claims will be officially cancelled, presuming that your recommendations are accepted?"

Moore pondered Clay's question for a moment. "It will take us until late summer to write our report, and make our formal recommendations. The BLM will initiate a Government Contest, the claim owners will respond, a trial will be held, and the administrative court will rule. I'd guess the whole process could take a year or two, maybe longer if there is an appeal to Washington. That answer your question?"

"Well, yes," Clay said, a note of resignation in his voice. "What is the status of our agate mining operation during all that time?"

"If you guys are presently mining agatized wood and bone, as you say you are, and if you sincerely believe that your claims are valid claims, then until the government finally decides otherwise, you can continue to operate your claims," Norris said. "But eventually you will lose them, I can guarantee you that. If you paid Menlove and Glover for those claims, I'd sure ask for my money back."

They all just stood there looking at each other. There didn't seem to be anything more to say. After a few moments, Wayne Moore broke the silence. "Well, I guess we've answered your questions. Maybe you ought to consult a lawyer. We can't stop the process, you know."

"Geez, Clay, what do you make of that?" Jerry sputtered as Moore and Norris drove off. "What are we going to do now?"

"Christ, I dunno," Clay replied, looking dejected. "This goddam project is falling apart, and I'm at a loss as to what to do next. Mr. George is already unhappy we can't find the diamond bonanza I guess he thought we would find. Menlove and Glover own mining claims covering the best prospecting ground and the BLM tells us that their mining claims are no good, and the whole area is going to be transferred to the Navajos. Wow."

"Well, by Geehosiphat," Jerry said, "I'm gonna mine all the agate, wood and bone I can haul out of here before the BLM lowers the boom on us! There won't be one scrap left for the Navajos. Not that they give a darn, anyhow."

"Yeah, that's about the only option left," Clay muttered, "We've got to speed up our operations, while I try to find a way around these obstacles."

Clay and Jerry then headed up to the trading post to talk with Jed Hatch. He was stacking canned goods on high wood shelves that lined the walls as they entered. "Well, you men sure sent a jolt through them BLM boys! That guy, Norris, he's a hard one to agitate, but you sure had him upset."

Jerry filled him in on their hostile meeting and then asked how many workers Jed could find in the local Navajo community. Jed thought about it, then started to name several he thought might be available. Jerry took notes and asked Jed to spread the word that he was hiring.

Clay then asked Jed who he should contact to get permission to continue prospecting after the land was transferred to the Navajos.

Jed shook his head. "The Navajo Nation has its headquarters down in Window Rock on the main reservation in northeastern Arizona. The only guy to talk to is Peter Begay, the tribal president. He's an important character, virtually runs the tribe singlehanded. Big revenues from oil have recently made the tribe wealthy, but all the wealth is kept at tribal headquarters. The northern Navajos who live in the Aneth Extension, where much of the wealth is being generated, get just a little and they're unhappy. Navajos, as a people, are dirt poor, live in dirt houses and most have no water or electricity. Most don't even speak English. The Navajo Tribe, as a governmental entity, is rich and very powerful. They've got air-conditioned offices, corporate airplanes and pay the officials fat salaries. You've got your work cut out for you, Clay, negotiating a deal with their tribal leader. Of course, even if you can work out a deal with Peter Begay, the deal still has to receive the approval of the feds at BIA. It's hard to get those two parties to agree on anything. Begay hates the BIA for interfering with his deals, and the BIA seems envious of Begay."

"You paint a pretty bleak picture, Jed. Haven't you got anything encouraging to say to me?" Clay asked.

"No. You're going to get a strong dose of how hard it is for an individual to do business with the Navajos. It seems only big oil companies can afford to do business on the reservation. You'll see."

Back at camp the three workers were waiting for a ride to Alkali Wash. Clay drove them up in the Jeep while Jerry stayed at camp to unload the pickup and hire more workers as soon as they showed up. Pete Shonto and his crew got busy while Clay prowled around the deposit pondering what Jed Hatch had said.

Mid-morning, as the workers took a breather, Clay waved Peter Shonto over. He offered him a drink from his canteen. "Pete," Clay said, "Have you heard of the Code Talkers?"

"Sure," Pete replied. "They're the pride of the Navajo Nation. I know several of them. I was in Europe during the war. They didn't use Code Talkers over there. Were you in the war?"

Clay explained that he had been a second lieutenant in the Army Air Force, trained to be a pilot, but eventually assigned as a flight navigator. It was flight training that first took him to Camp Kearns near Salt Lake City and introduced him to the Rocky Mountains and the West. It was love at first encounter, Clay said, and he decided to spend his life in the outdoors in the West. After the war ended he attended college on the GI Bill and got degrees in geology from Amherst College. When he was offered a job with the U.S. Geological Survey in western Colorado, he jumped at the offer and wound up working on the Colorado Plateau based out of Grand Junction, Colorado. That's where he first met Jerry Brooks, he concluded.

"I was a corporal in the infantry in Europe," Pete said, "And after the war I went to college on the GI Bill, too. I took accounting and business classes, but I didn't stay through graduation. My elderly parents wanted me back home on the reservation, so I came back. Farming and herding sheep didn't appeal to me, so I've hired myself out on various jobs, mining, shop keeping, road construction, truck driver. Finding employment on the reservation is difficult. The oil companies are starting to hire Navajos, so maybe things will improve."

"What do you know about Peter Begay?" Clay asked.

"Not much," Pete answered, "He has been tribal leader for several years, and he is responsible for many improvements on the reservation. He is a very popular leader on the main reservation. I hear he is very smart. I know he graduated from college, but I never met him. That's all I know," he said.

At noon Jerry drove up in the pickup loaded with six Navajos. He assigned two to work the rocker under Clay's supervision and the others were added to Pete Shonto's crew. As they sat eating lunch, Jerry said, "Jed thinks he can find me a couple more men, but then we've about exhausted the local labor pool. I got to thinking about us being forced off the claims and I decided to stockpile fossil material somewhere else, probably Blanding. Somewhere off the reservation, on private land. This stuff is mighty valuable."

"How are our finances holding up?" Clay asked. "All these men, and the hauling expenses, it's got to add up. I'll write a check for my half."

"That's what I like, a partner anxious to write checks," Jerry laughed. "I'll work up some figures tonight after supper. But I tell you, Clay, for every dollar it's costing us, we're gonna make $10, or more. You'll be able to afford that airplane in no time! How you doing finding diamonds?"

"Not very good at all," Clay replied as he thought about their predicament.

Testing cemented gravel in buried stream channels was slow, costly and so far not very productive. Tunneling along the fossil channels into the canyon walls was theoretically possible, but would be costly and there wasn't much chance of blundering into a valuable pocket of diamonds. Selective mining on a small scale, as could be done along a thin vein of gold ore, wouldn't be very productive here since there wasn't any vein structure or deposit to follow, except the broad stream channel. It wasn't very likely mining a fossil stream channel would ever be a paying proposition, unless he could figure out how diamonds might have been concentrated by stream action. So far, he didn't have any ideas. Mining on a vastly increased scale, extracting every bit of gravel in the entire channel for processing to recover diamonds, would require enormous capital commitments and years to accomplish. Unless he could figure out how to drive a small tunnel directly to an accumulation of alluvial diamonds, Clay thought their small diamond mining venture was doomed to failure. About all he could do for now was to process the gravel produced by Jerry's fossil mining operations and recover any diamonds the gravel contained. That's what he intended to do for the foreseeable future, or until he came up with a better idea.

As the days passed, Jerry's stockpiles of agatized wood and bone grew. Jerry posted one of his workers to guard his stockpiles at night, after he noticed some strange tire marks leading up to one of his piles. Clay's two-man crew broke lumps of cemented gravel and ran the rocker to wash the piles of gravel produced by Jerry's crews. At night, down by the creek at their camp, Clay and Jerry lamped the rocker concentrates for large diamonds, and panned for the smaller diamonds. Clay's collection of diamonds picked out of the rocker and pan concentrates was becoming respectable, but still nothing to get very excited about.

Clay had run across two more small pockets, but he still couldn't figure how they had accumulated at a particular spot.

One day in late April, Clay and Jerry got word that Charlie Nevilles was now back in Blanding so they decided to pay him a visit. They still needed to settle up with him on the camping equipment. They picked a Sunday when their crews weren't working. They arrived just before noon.

"Well, how are you gentlemen doing?" Charlie said as they got out. "Been down on the reservation, I hear."

"We came to settle up on the equipment we helped ourselves to," Clay said, laughing.

"How about $150 a week?" Charlie said.

"A bargain," Clay replied with a grin. "How long can we keep it?"

"Well, I'll need the cooking gear for a trip in June. I doubt if I'll need the big tent until mid-summer," he said. "How long are you guys going to be camped out?"

"Probably not much longer than late May," Jerry spoke up, "Unless Clay here can get us an extension from the tribe. The BLM is trying to kick us off and our long term prospects aren't good at all. I need your advice about finding a place here in Blanding to store some valuable materials we're mining."

"Well, I've been thinking about expanding my storage facilities and I'll have lots of extra room, at least in the beginning. I'd be pleased to rent you all the fenced space you'll need. Any really valuable stuff can be put in a large shed I'm going to set up. Of course, Nancy and the kids are here every day for added security."

After Jerry and Charlie worked out the details, Charlie turned to Clay. "Aren't you going to ask me how the lady tourists made out after we dropped you guys off ?"

"Uh, sure," Clay replied, wondering what Charlie had up his sleeve.

"Them ladies sure pined after you fellows left us, especially that pretty one, Sandy Logan. She sure was impressed with you, Clay, and asked me to give you this note when I saw you next." He smiled broadly as he handed Clay a piece of paper. Clay unfolded the note, blushing.

"Now," Clay stammered. "how did the rest of the trip go?" trying to change the subject.

"Our camp that night was a sorry affair and for the next two days it was wet, windy and cold. Even Chester's cooking couldn't make up for the dismal weather. When we finally got out at Crossing of the Fathers, we had to wait for almost two days for Smiley to show up with the van and the boat trailer. He'd had a breakdown driving over and was late arriving. Then, while we were camped out at the disembarkation point, here came Georgie White and one of her enormous Colorado River rafting groups. I didn't know anyone else was on the river that early in the season. I think there must have been 75 people in her group, all wet and tired. It looked like a refugee camp on the Colorado River. Our ladies complained that once you guys left the group, it wasn't fun any more. I had to agree."

"They missed us, did they?" Jerry laughed. "Did Art catch any more catfish?"

"No, even the catfishing dropped off after you guys left," Charlie said. "We were reduced to eating canned Spam for breakfast that last day."

Clay then asked to use the telephone to call Mr. George in Los Angeles. He reported to him the progress to date and the deteriorating land situation. He asked for another meeting and they set a time for a meeting in Salt Lake. Clay urged him to get an appointment with Milton S. Lassiter, a prominent mining lawyer with offices in Clay's building.

Clay and Jerry then said their goodbyes to the Nevilles and headed over to the Town Cafe for a late afternoon Sunday dinner before returning to camp.

A fossil mine operation at the alkali wash deposit.

11

SUCCESS AND PROBLEMS

The Navajo work crew, now consisting of eleven workers, appeared at the field camp early Monday morning, ready to be driven to Alkali Wash for a busy day. Jerry loaded six of them into his pickup truck and Clay took the other five in his Jeep. By eight o'clock the air compressor was roaring, and everyone was busy.

Around mid-morning a loaded farm truck drove up and two men got out. One was a smiling Charlie Nevilles.

"So this is what you boys have been up to for the past few weeks," he said over the roar of the compressor. Clay motioned them away from the noise as Jerry joined them. They shook hands and Charlie introduced Smiley Kerr, a Blanding farmer who worked for Charlie.

"We're headed for Bluff," Charlie said, "but since we're about two hours ahead of the main group, I decided to stop over and tell you what arrangements I was able to make yesterday and to introduce you to Smiley. Jed Hatch told us where we could find you." Pointing to the farm truck, Charlie continued, "This is the truck Smiley will haul your stuff up to my place in, if you want to hire him. Can you take a minute to show him what it is you want him to haul?"

Jerry then walked Smiley around, pointing out how each pile needed to be kept separate. Jerry asked him to bring down some boards and nails on his first trip, so they could construct boxes to hold the semi-precious agate materials. Jerry planned to put the boxes of agate in the shed. The petrified logs and bones would be just fine outside.

Charlie looked at his watch. "We gotta get moving. We need to be in Bluff when the van and boat trailer arrives. Smiley can be here tomorrow morning, if it's okay with you."

Jerry suggested he make it Friday instead and thanked Charlie for his assistance, wishing him a good trip down the river. Charlie and Smiley then got in, backed up the truck, and headed Hatch.

As the truck disappeared from sight, Jerry turned to Clay. "I sure am impressed with how helpful these southeastern Utah folks can be. Jed Hatch has been a godsend in dealing with these Navajos, and now Charlie Nevilles is coming to our assistance. It sure is neighborly."

"You're right," replied Clay, "but it's also good business. When Jed and Charlie step forward like they did, it makes them look good in the eyes of their neighbors. It's often like that in a small community."

There was a lot of progress in the Alkali Wash operation over the next few days. Jerry had now collected tons of petrified logs, well over two tons of large agatized dinosaur bones, and a sizable collection of the semi-precious agatized bone and wood chunks, all carefully arranged in piles and boxes. Clay even had two small bottles of diamonds, about eight ounces he estimated, and a small cotton bag nearly filled with small fragments. It was time to plan a trip to Salt Lake City, to meet with Mr. George and for Jerry to visit his family.

Jerry instructed Pete Shonto about what to do in his absence and got Smiley Kerr hauling material up to Nevilles' storage yard. They expected to be gone for only four or five days, but they didn't want things to slow down. They decided to take Jerry's pickup loaded with semi-precious agate, leaving the Jeep for Pete to drive the crews out to Alkali Wash each day.

Since Clay's appointment with Mr. George was Tuesday, they decided to start the long drive Saturday morning, expecting to arrive in Salt Lake City late that evening. Jerry wanted to spend Sunday with his family and Clay would use Sunday and Monday to take care of his personal business.

They left at dawn and when they stopped in Moab for lunch at the Trail Cafe, there was Dick Norman reading his newspaper over his lunch. He was surprised and pleased to see them walk in, so they joined him.

The big news was that the Atomic Energy Commission had announced plans to terminate its guaranteed ore buying program, but everyone in the uranium business was sure this would lead to hot competition among electric utilities who, until now, could buy their nuclear power plant fuel from the AEC at controlled prices. This news was seen as a prologue to better things to come. Jerry listened in disbelief. Clay asked Dick if he knew anything about the big oil strike down near Aneth, but Dick didn't know anything about it, and didn't seem to take it seriously.

Clay and Jerry finished a hasty lunch, and said so long to Dick. Back on the road, they passed through Crescent Junction and on through Green River and finally after a long boring drive they entered the coal mining communities of Wellington and Price. As they entered Price from the southeast, they chuckled over a roadside sign:

Next Time Fly
Green River Flying Service

"That must be Jim Hewitt's," Clay chuckled. They stopped for gas and inquired about the condition of the highway over Soldier Summit and down Spanish Fork Canyon into Provo and the valley of Utah Lake. The news was ominous: a wet spring snowstorm with blowing snow the whole way. The high plateau terrain of Soldier Summit could be really bad when there was blowing snow, and since storms came in from the west, the report meant the Wasatch Front was likely to be nasty that night. Jerry was glad his pickup truck was loaded since it had better snow traction with lots of weight over the rear tires. They continued on, climbing up Price Canyon, headed for the 8,000 foot summit.

On top of the plateau the wind-whipped snow blotted out the asphalt roadway in places, and blinded Jerry to oncoming traffic. He drove slowly ahead until he reached the summit and started down winding Spanish Fork Canyon. The road was greasy with wet snow and several semi-trailer trucks had slipped off the highway, one lying on its side. Other trucks and automobiles had stopped beside the highway, afraid to proceed, but Jerry continued on.

After an hour they emerged onto the flat terrain of Utah Valley, but the snowstorm continued. Highway traffic was light that evening since anyone with brains was safe in his home on such a bad night.

Finally, about ten o'clock they crossed Point of the Mountain and entered the valley of the Great Salt Lake and could see the lights of Salt Lake City ahead. They were home. Jerry drove Clay to his house in the lower Avenues District, promising to call the next afternoon. Jerry then headed to his home in Sugarhouse.

Clay stomped up the snowy porch stairs and unlocked the front door. A large pile of unopened mail on the floor behind the mail slot reminded him how long he had been away.

Sunday morning dawned white and crisp, with about eight inches of new snow on Clay's small lawn. As the bright morning sun rose over the snowy Wasatch Mountains to the east and illuminated the equally snowy Oquirrh Range to the southwest, Clay marveled at how weather could change so quickly in the Mountain West, and how new snow made everything look so beautiful. He felt good, just thinking of where he was.

Without his Jeep and with an empty cupboard, Clay decided to trudge down to a neighborhood store for some groceries. Downtown Salt Lake, only a few blocks from his home, would be deserted on a snowy Sunday morning, and the small grocery market wouldn't open until noon on a Sunday, so he was forced to change his plans. It was only three blocks in a different direction to Bill's Cafe, a breakfast spot sure to be open. He could pick up a Sunday newspaper to read over breakfast.

By mid-afternoon Clay had restocked his larder, sorted his mail, and was reading some magazines when the telephone rang. It was Blaine George, confirming that they were meeting on schedule. He would be flying in from Los Angeles on Monday, staying at the Newhouse Hotel as usual. He said that he had gotten a Tuesday morning appointment with the mining attorney that Clay had recommended. He proposed meeting Clay, and Jerry if he could make it, for dinner at the hotel on Monday evening.

After he hung up, Clay realized Mr. George hadn't even asked about their diamond mining. Most strange, he thought to himself.

Jerry called late Sunday afternoon, as promised, and Clay told him about the dinner invitation. "Do I have to?" Jerry whined in fake despair.

"Of course not," Clay said, "But don't make a decision now. We'll have lots of time to discuss things tomorrow. Can you come by and take me with you to your shop in the morning? I want to be there to see Mary's face when she sees the agate."

"Too late," Jerry laughed, "She's already taken a look and called some local dealers and lapidarists to come down to the shop and pick out some of the best. You'll get your kicks watching those guys go ape over our stuff. I tell you, Clay, we've got a real fortune."

132

The next morning Jerry and Mary pulled up in front of Clay's house and honked the horn. Clay pulled on his coat and hurried out, crowding into the warm cab with them. When they got to the rock shop a small crowd had already gathered at the front door. Mary let them in while Jerry took the truck to the back. They all hurried in as Jerry peeled away the tarpaulin covering the load. There was a collective gasp when they saw all the material. There was a buying frenzy and in less than an hour the bed of the pickup truck was empty. Clay and Jerry stood there, stunned at how the crowd had snapped up what they viewed as a great bargain. Mary was busy at the cash register, tallying sales.

"Man, was I ever right!" Jerry chortled. "See how those folks reacted to our material? We could have charged twice as much and they still would have cleaned us out!"

"It seemed like some of them wanted more," Clay said. "What did Mary charge them for this load?"

"Like I said a few days ago, a flat $15 per pound," Jerry replied. "I estimate we had about 1500 pounds. At $15 a pound that calculates to $22,500. Say $20,000 to be conservative. See what I've been talking about?"

Clay nodded in stunned silence. Gee whiz, we're wasting our time looking for diamonds, he thought to himself.

When everyone had left, Jerry and Clay tallied up the actual sales, which came to $22,125 for a total of 1,475 pounds of agatized bone. That money would cover a lot of costs and still leave plenty left over. And there was even more yet to be mined.

Clay then asked Jerry to give him a lift to his office, so he could check his mail and telephone calls. On the drive over, Jerry said he was feeling much too excited to meet with Mr. George.

"But I'd like to attend your conference with the lawyer," Jerry said. "I need to get educated and be in a position to figure out how we can keep operating, no matter what. I ain't about to just walk away from our own little gold mine in Alkali Wash, no sirree!"

It was late Monday morning when Clay opened the door to his office. Jeanie was sitting at her desk, typing. "Hi, boss," she said as Clay closed the door behind him. "It's been a long time since I last saw you. You look mighty pleased. Good News?"

"Jeanie, my little dove," Clay said, patting her on the top of her head, "Today I am one happy boss! How about I take you to lunch, somewhere exclusive, like Dan's Meat Pies up the street at the billiard parlor?"

"Are you drunk?" she asked. "Or just delusional? You know I don't eat meat. What gives?"

"Neither drunk nor delusional. I'm rich!" Clay almost shouted. "At least, I'm about to be rich. Actually, I guess I'm financially secure at last, and on the verge of becoming much more so. I guess that means I'm rich, I think."

"Gee, boss, you used to make sense, but now, I dunno," she said, looking at him. "If you want to spend some of your money, sure you can take me to lunch, but let's go to the salad bar over at the hotel."

After lunch where the salad bar cost more than Clay's steak sandwich, they returned to the office. Jeanie, a social studies student at the University of Utah, had a side business typing term papers using Clay's IBM electric typewriter and office equipment, and she had a tight deadline to meet. Clay had lots of unopened business mail, and many telephone calls to return, so they busied themselves for the rest of the afternoon, until Jeanie said that it was nearly five and she had to catch a bus up to the university.

Clay looked at his pile of unfinished business and sighed in frustration. He telephoned Mr. George at the hotel and informed him that Jerry wouldn't be able to join them for dinner. Mr. George invited Clay to join him in the Roof Restaurant for a cocktail before dinner.

"You know, Utah has some queer liquor laws," Clay said. "You can't just order an alcoholic drink, especially a mixed drink or cocktail. I belong to a private club just across the intersection from the hotel. We can get a cocktail there. I'll meet you in the lobby at six."

Clay then placed a quick call to the Manhattan Club. Monday wasn't a big drinking day among club members, but the establishment was open for business as usual.

Mr. George was sitting in a large chair in the lobby as Clay walked in. "Good to see you again, Clay," he said in a warm tone.

Well, Clay thought to himself, he seems more relaxed than the last time.

They walked across the intersection and down an outside stairwell under a garish street level neon sign reading Manhattan Club with an arrow pointing down. The place was completely empty except for a bartender and a waitress talking at the bar. As Clay and Mr. George settled into a rear corner table, Clay fumbled for his wallet and produced a small membership card. She inspected it carefully, then handed it back.

Clay turned to George. "What's your poison? The bartender can probably mix anything you want."

"How about a Manhattan," George replied. "That should be perfect since it's the name of your club. Make it a double."

"I'll have a tall gin and tonic," Clay said.

"I've had a cocktail at the Alta Club and it wasn't such a bother. What is the situation here? Tell me about Utah's liquor laws," George said.

Clay explained that private social clubs, like the Alta Club, are somewhat different from commercial privately owned clubs, like the Manhattan Club. Clay told him how the Mormon-dominated Utah Legislature years ago had established a state-controlled monopoly for the sale and dispensing of liquor that prohibited the sale of spirituous drinks in public establishments.

"In order to buy liquor in Utah, even for personal use, you need to be officially registered with the State Liquor Control Commission, which is intended to discourage secret drinking by Mormons. The gentiles, that is, the non-Mormons, raised a howl," Clay continued, "so the legislature authorized a limited number of private social clubs to allow drinking away from one's home. Initially the private social clubs were cooperatives, owned by the members, but soon certain enterprising individuals formed private clubs run for profit. The local police tightly control the licensing of all private clubs, and shut them down if they allow non-members on the premises. Except guests of members, of course. In Salt Lake the police sometimes send decoys, non-members, to test a club's security practices. This private club is a real money-maker for the owner, so he has his people check memberships carefully. I don't come here often enough to be recognized, and you are a stranger. It's something you have to get used to, living here."

"So I can't have an alcoholic drink in a public establishment in Utah, unless I belong to a private club?" Mr. George asked.

"Not exactly," Clay replied. "You can bring your own booze in a paper bag to most any restaurant, and pour yourself a drink. That's called brown bagging. It's all very complicated, and especially confusing to visitors. That's why a visitor to Utah needs a local guide. That's why you've got me."

Clay then carefully pulled out his two small bottles of diamonds, and poured them out on a white paper napkin. "So far this is all we've found for all our efforts," he said. "I've got about five ounces of small fragments at home, stuff that probably has value for industrial purposes. I'll give you the bag tomorrow when we meet with the lawyer. I'm not sure what these larger stones are worth, but I think their value will cover your expenses for Jerry and me. It isn't much of a commercial incentive to your investors. I've been trying to figure out how these stones might have become concentrated in pockets or could be found in quantity, but, frankly, I haven't been successful." He sat back to observe Mr. George's reaction.

Mr. George looked around, but the club was still empty. He inspected each stone closely, then placed them back in the bottles. "Most of them aren't very big, are they?" he said.

Clay thought for a moment. "I'm delighted to have found the source, which I really doubted could be found in southeastern Utah or on the Navajo reservation. But, as you recognized, finding the geological source isn't the same as finding a profitable deposit. I haven't been able to do that, and right now I don't think I ever will."

"But where did those gemstones in my jewelry come from?" Mr. George asked. "How could the Navajos find such stones, but you can't?"

"I've been thinking about that, myself," Clay replied. "I've concluded that those old Navajos must have blundered into a rich pocket, perhaps only a single pocket, and created the few pieces you purchased. In other words, we're dealing with a mineral curiosity, not a mineral deposit. The fact that those ancient Navajos found any diamonds at all is amazing. It's possible that if we kept looking, we might be able to find a similar pocket ourselves. But one or two pockets of diamonds won't make a modern mining venture pay. That's the sad truth, I think."

"Let's go have dinner, Clay," Mr. George said after a long pause, "We'll see what the lawyer says tomorrow. Maybe his advice will put a new light on our project."

The next morning Jerry came to Clay's office, and a few minutes before eleven Mr. George joined them and they all took the elevator to the tenth floor offices of Lassiter & Bown. Entering the frosted glass double entry doors carrying the name of the law firm, they approached the prominent desk of an elderly woman. "Can I help you?" she said, looking up.

"Mr. George, Mr. Greer and Mr. Brooks, to see Mr. Lassiter," Mr. George said. "We have an eleven o'clock appointment."

Consulting an appointment book, she pointed to a row of straight backed wooden chairs lining the entry area. "Please be seated. Mr. Lassiter is with a client and will be with you shortly."

Clay and Jerry seated themselves, while Mr. George remained standing, looking around the office at the glass-fronted bookcases containing vintage law books. The base of each bookcase was a multi-tiered set of small drawers which Mr. George opened and inspected. The elderly secretary looked at Mr. George with disapproval, but said nothing.

After what seemed a long time, actually only 20 minutes, the door to Lassiter's office opened and several people could be seen standing and shaking hands.

The first person to exit the office was a short, rotund silver-haired man with a rosy pink complexion and an imperious air, followed closely by a slim young man in a dark suit. Clay recognized the rotund man as Federal District Judge Willis A. Ritter, a man of great reputation in the community. As Judge Ritter walked past them, he looked closely at Mr. George, but ignored Clay and Jerry. After Judge Ritter and his shadow had passed through the glass doors and into the outside corridor, Clay turned and saw a tall, slender gray haired man standing in the open office door, talking to the elderly secretary. As Clay watched, the tall man turned and looked at them.

He waived them in, as the elderly secretary said, "Mr. Lassiter will see you now." Mr. George entered the large office first, and took a center seat still warm from the presence of Judge Ritter. Clay took a chair on the far side of Mr. George's chair, near a window, and Jerry sat in an chair near the door. Another young man in a dark business suit was sitting in a chair on the end of Mr. Lassiter's large desk. He had a long yellow legal pad before him.

"What can I do for you, er..," Mr. Lassiter said, looking at a piece of paper handed to him by his secretary, "...Mr. George?" He looked around the room, then focused on Mr. George as he spoke up to introduce Clay and Jerry.

Mr. Lassiter was about 65 and wore rimless glasses. He seemed to be in frail health, but not the least lacking in vigor. Clay thought he detected a faint stutter. Original art hung on walls beside and behind his desk and a carved wooden duck decoy sat on his desk. Otherwise the room was a typical lawyer's office of the times with law books in glass-fronted bookcases lining one entire wall.

Mr. George then asked Clay to explain the situation at Montezuma Creek and Alkali Wash, the situation of the mining claims, the BLM's mining claim investigation, and the pending transfer of federal lands to the Navajo reservation. Clay had been cautioned not to mention gemstones or diamonds. The young man at the end of Mr. Lassiter's large desk wrote furiously as Clay talked.

As Clay concluded his explanation, Mr. Lassiter thought for a moment. "Gentlemen, I am thoroughly aware of what Mr. Greer is describing, and of your dilemma. Mr. Greer, you say you are mining is a deposit of petrified wood and dinosaur bone? BLM policy is that fossils are not a locatable mineral deposit, did you know that? I doubt that BLM will find your claims valid."

"Yes, sir, we know that," Clay replied. "But our deposit contains semi-precious agatized bone and wood, valuable in jewelry manufacture. Doesn't that make a difference? What did the BLM guys mean when they referred to a with-drawal date?"

Mr. Lassiter filled them in on the U.S. Mining Law and BLM's enforce-ment role. Mostly he confirmed the information and opinions Wayne Moore and Hu Norris had given Clay and Jerry two weeks ago, but it was helpful to hear the information again, told in slightly different terms, by a disinterested professional. Lassiter certainly seemed to know his business, Clay thought to himself. He was glad that Mr. George was there.

When Lassiter had finished, Mr. George spoke up. "Given our circum-stances and the current laws, what do you recommend as the best course of action? We want to continue to exploit these deposits if we can."

"Under the circumstances, your best course is to negotiate with the Na-vajo tribe for a mining lease or concession. Isn't it better to pay a royalty to those who will have good title to the lands, than to pay a royalty to mining claim owners whose claims are under attack and who will almost certainly lose in a battle with the BLM?" Turning to Jerry, he asked, "How much royalty do you currently pay the claim owners?"

Jerry said, "Ten cents a pound." Lassiter looked surprised, and quietly chuckled. "I don't think the Navajos will accept such a low royalty for semi-precious agate. I think I see your dilemma more clearly, now," he said.

Mr. George then thanked Mr. Lassiter for his advice and requested that a bill be sent to him at his office in Los Angeles, handing him a business card.

Seated around Clay's desk back in his office, Mr. George said, "Clay, I think the next order of business is for you to visit the officers of the Navajo tribe and see what kind of a lease or concession we can negotiate. You negotiated an awfully good lease from those claim owners. I think you will do quite all right by yourself."

"I'm not very optimistic about negotiating with the Navajos," Clay said. "Are we prepared to enter into a long term, expensive arrangement, particularly in view of our inability to find commercial diamond deposits?"

Mr. George thought for a minute. "Clay, see if you can negotiate a contract with them that gives us plenty of time to explore and evaluate what we find, with an option to receive a long term lease if we are successful. Of course, before you commit to anything, call me. Negotiate in your name, personally, until we find out what they're willing to do. Keep my name and my investor group completely out of the picture."

Turning to Jerry, Mr. George said, "Can you drive me to the airport? There's a flight to Los Angeles leaving in about an hour that will get me to Los Angeles tonight."

Jerry nodded, and Mr. George left to collect his bag at the hotel. Clay asked Jerry to come back to the office after he dropped Mr. George off.

Waiting for Jerry's return, Clay sorted through his mail and some telephone callback slips. One message caused him to stop in his tracks. "Hey, Jeanie," he called to the outer office. "Is this call from John Arcarius real? Or are you playing a joke on me?"

Jeanie appeared at his door. "No, boss, I don't kid. He called while you were at the lawyer's office. He sounded like he was an old friend."

"Yeah, I know him. Did he say what the call was about?"

"Only that it was very important for you to call him today," she said. "I told him you were going out of town tomorrow."

Clay sat down and dialed the number. "Mr. Arcarius, this is Clay Greer. I have a message to call you. To what do I owe the pleasure of your call?" After a short response, Clay replied, "Sure, if it's so important. I'm in my office right now, and I can meet with you in an hour, if that's convenient." The other party talked for a minute, then Clay said goodbye and hung up.

Minutes later Jerry walked into the office.

"Jerry, you'll never guess who just called me," Clay said. Jerry shrugged in puzzlement, so Clay continued, "My old nemesis the evil promoter, John S. Arcarius. You've heard me talk about him. He's coming over in about an hour. Do you think he's found out about our project?"

"I dunno, buddy," Jerry replied, "But you're gonna find out real soon. Me, I'm gonna go shopping for supplies. Tell me how it turns out." Jerry promptly left.

Clay looked anxiously around and decided to remove some project maps pinned on the wall and file away any papers that might give a curious visitor ideas. Arcarius was a notorious deal breaker and it wouldn't do have him pick up some tidbit about Clay's business, or the business of Clay's clients. He felt like a fool, inviting Arcarius to his office.

Promptly at three John S. Arcarius arrived, resplendent in his long camel hair overcoat with black velvet collar, looking like a millionaire businessman. He was a tall, handsome man with abundant black hair cut in the latest style. He reeked of importance and wealth. He introduced himself to Jeanie, who was greatly impressed, and spotting Clay at his desk, said in a loud friendly voice, "Clay, old friend, how nice of you to see me on such short notice. Your girl tells me that you are off to the field tomorrow. Anything exciting?"

You may fool some people, you slimy bastard, but you make my skin crawl, Clay thought to himself.

"What's so important that you needed to see me today?" Clay said, watching Arcarius' face closely.

"Ah, always the strictly business professional. That's why I admire you so," Arcarius said, too complimentary to be believable. "How much do you know about recent oil developments down in San Juan County?"

Clay remained impassive. "Not much. I'm mostly a mining geologist, you know."

"Yes, of course I know," Arcarius replied. "Well, some big oil companies

140

are drilling and finding oil near Aneth on the Navajo Indian Reservation. The news apparently hasn't gotten to Salt Lake yet, but some of my associates in northern New Mexico alerted me and I've come up with a plan to get in on the action. I'll need your professional help. I understand you're working in southern San Juan County on river gravel deposits, so perhaps you can help me and profit yourself at the same time."

Clay felt a prickly sensation in the nape of his neck. How in heck could he know that, Clay thought to himself. "What do you want me to do?" he said.

"I've convinced the director of the Utah State Land Board, a bridge partner of mine at my social club, that the San Juan River near Aneth qualifies as a navigable river, which means the State of Utah owns the bed of the river, not the Navajos. I have applied, through a confidential agent, for oil & gas leases from the State Land Board covering the entire bed of the San Juan River where it runs through the new Aneth oil field. My friend on the board informs me that mining claims in the bed of the San Juan River could impact the state's claim of title unless, of course, we also control those mining claims. The big oil companies will be in a panic when they find out that I hold oil & gas leases from the State of Utah on the entire bed of the river, and that the Navajos don't legally own it. I think they will pay handsomely to buy out my leases, and I don't want some technicality to becloud the State's title."

John Arcarius sounded downright moralistic as he spoke, and Clay's blood curdled at the audacity of this latest scam. He was offended that Arcarius would consider him for a part in any scheme, but Clay was determined to listen him out.

"Where do I fit into this scheme?" Clay asked.

"I want you to plaster the entire San Juan River with placer mining claims in the names of persons I will supply to you," Arcarius said. "You know all about mining claims on river deposits and how to locate them properly. These would be association placer mining claims, and I have no experience with such claims. I am informed that you are very knowledgeable."

"How do you know that?" Clay asked, curious.

Arcarius hesitated. "Oh, I have some mining associates in Green River who follow your activities quite closely."

Holy Jesus, Clay thought to himself almost aloud, this guy is in cahoots with the Baker Brothers. He might even know about our search for diamonds.

What in heck am I going to do now? His brain raced for some means of dealing with this sudden and unexpected development, while maintaining a calm demeanor.

"The whole scheme doesn't make sense to me," Clay said in a seemingly disinterested tone. "How could locating mining claims on the river bed affect the state's title? I thought the whole area was withdrawn by the feds from locating new mining claims and the BLM is out in the field canceling any claims that existed before the withdrawal." After a moments reflection, he added, "Anyhow, lands owned by the State of Utah aren't open to location of mining claims under federal laws. I never get involved in anything that I think doesn't make sense."

Arcarius leaned forward. "It will all make perfect sense if everything is done exactly as I direct, and if you carry out the claim locations exactly as I say. Your name need not be associated with the operation, if that is your wish. I will supply all of the paperwork, claim names and dates of location, the names of the claim locators, and all the other details. All I want is someone competent like yourself to carry out my precise instructions."

Clay stared at Arcarius across his desk, his mind racing at the implications of what Arcarius had just said. He thought to himself, *Geez, I think I know what this rascal is up to. He's going to fabricate ancient placer mining claims on the bed of the San Juan River and then assert that these phony claims predated establishment of the Aneth Extension. That would assure that the Navajo's rights wouldn't attach to the river bed until after it was classified as a navigable river. He probably has some plan to relinquish the phony claims after the state's title to the bed of the river is formally declared navigable, whatever that means. No wonder he is so determined to enlist someone qualified to properly locate the claim monuments and place the false paper notices on the ground. A slipup in monumenting and papering the bogus mining claims could cause the claims to be questioned and the whole house of cards could collapse. Golly, what a devious mind,* Clay marveled. *The man was a genius gone awry.* Clay decided to hide behind the Conflict of Interest shield.

"Mr. Arcarius, you know perfectly well that I am still retained by the Texas investor group that you are still attempting to do business with," he said sternly. "I can't accept employment from you on any matter, whether it is related to their business or not."

"Oh," Arcarius said weakly, "I thought you'd find some way around that little problem. You would be most handsomely compensated for your participation, you understand. And, as I said, your name wouldn't be associated with it in any way." He could see from the steely look in Clay's eyes that this plea had fallen on deaf ears. "Well, I trust to your professionalism that you won't say anything about this conversation to anyone."

"If you mean, will I run to Texaco or Superior Oil with news of your scheme, of course I won't," he replied. "But if I were to be subpoenaed as a witness in a lawsuit, I'd have to tell what I know."

John S. Arcarius paled, stunned to realize that Clay was aware of the oil companies who actually held leases at Aneth. "Trust me, Mr. Greer, you will never be subpoenaed in a lawsuit. I will guarantee that." With that, he hastily left the office.

Good riddance, Clay thought as he followed Arcarius to the doorway and watched him get on the elevator. As he turned around, Jeanie gave him a knowing look. "A bad character, Huh? Why is it all the fancy dressers turn out to be bad characters? He sure could have fooled me!"

Yeah, Clay thought to himself, that's why guys like him are so successful at working their scams. If you want to succeed as a con man you've got to look prosperous.

"Well, Jeanie," he replied, "You must learn not to be deceived by appearances. That guy is a slimy character who fools a lot of people, but I know him for what he really is."

"Well, you certainly sent him running. What did you say to him?"

Clay smiled. "I just let him know I was on to his scam and that I didn't want any part in it. I also let him know I could blow the whistle on him, if he didn't behave."

"Are there many guys like him in the mining business?" Jeanie asked.

"There are too many like him in every business," Clay replied. "Mining and the oil business depend on some enthusiastic individual to get things started. These individuals are generally called promoters and such a label ought to be honorable. But crooked promoters are far too numerous in my business. They give our whole business a bad name."

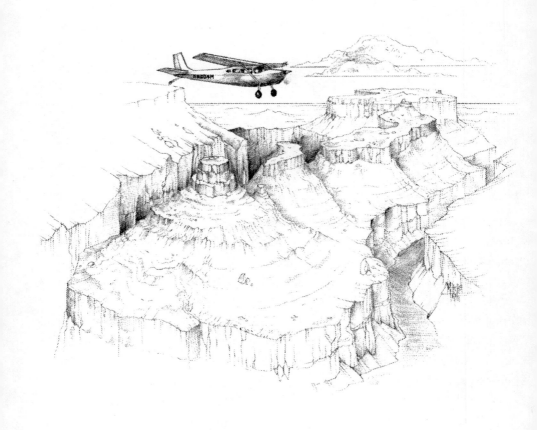

Cessna 180 in flight over canyon country.

12

WINDOW ROCK

The following morning Clay and Jerry began the long trip back to Hatch Trading Post. They got an early start, hoping to drive straight through and arrive at their camp by late evening.

On the way Clay told Jerry about his meeting with John Arcarius and his worries about dealing with the Navajos.

When they got to the coal mining town of Price, Clay decided to telephone the Navajo tribal offices in Window Rock, Arizona, to see if he could schedule an appointment with the tribal president. The only opening was tomorrow afternoon. Clay mumbled that he would try to get there, but in his heart he didn't know how he could possibly make it.

Clay and Jerry made plans as they headed south toward Moab. Jerry agreed that driving straight through to Window Rock was barely possible. Then Jerry had an idea. "Maybe your friend Jim Hewitt can fly you down. We're driving right through Green River. I'm sure your client won't mind the expense under these conditions."

When they reached the hanger office, Sandy Hewitt looked up from her cluttered desk.

"Hi, Sandy," Clay said, "Does Jim have an opening in his schedule tomorrow morning?" He had noticed that Jim's Cessna 180 was nowhere to be seen.

"Clay, its good to see you. Jim flew into Grand Junction for some parts, but he doesn't have anything scheduled for tomorrow. You want me to pencil you in?"

"You bet," Clay replied with a broad smile. "When is Jim due back?"

"Should be back by dusk," Sandy replied. "The weather is marginal, but it improves as you head south. It might be a tad better tomorrow. Where are you headed?"

"I need to be in Window Rock tomorrow afternoon," Clay replied. Sandy and Clay then examined a large aeronautical chart on the office wall, found Window Rock, and noted a small airstrip in the valley right next to the community. "The Navajo tribe has a small fleet of corporate aircraft they keep at the nearby municipal airport in Gallup, New Mexico. I'm surprised that they don't have a bigger airport at their headquarters," Sandy said.

"I'm sure that's next," Jerry chimed in, laughing.

Clay and Jerry then settled down in the Hewitt's small office to await Jim's return. They asked Sandy about the Navajo tribe, but about all she seemed to know was they had quite a fleet of twin engined airplanes, the envy of even the rich oil companies operating in the region.

About an hour before dark Jim taxied up and killed the engine. Clay was outside before the propeller stopped rotating. Jim Hewitt got out, surprised to see Clay and Jerry again.

"You guys back on more business, I hope," Jim said.

"You bet," Clay said. "I need you to fly me down to Window Rock for a meeting with the tribal president in the early afternoon. Nancy says the weather looks okay. Can you hang around and fly me back to Blanding after my meeting?"

"My, things must be getting exciting if you're meeting with the Navajo bosses," Jim said. "Clay, you present yourself here in the morning, and I'll take care of the rest."

Clay and Jim spent the night at the Green Well Motel and after a hearty breakfast the next morning at the Trailside Cafe, Jerry dropped Clay off at Jim Hewitt's hanger and left for Blanding. He promised to meet Clay at the Blanding airport around four. Jim and Clay climbed into the Cessna 180 and taxied out to the landing strip.

Takeoff was to the east, away from the center of town. Jim then turned due south, flying along the course of the Green River. It was impossible to carry on a conversation in the noisy airplane, so Clay contented himself with looking out at the panorama unfolding below them.

The Green River carved an increasingly deep and narrow valley, but below the mouth of the San Rafael River the channel became a narrow winding vertical-walled canyon, slicing through thousands of feet of sandstone cliffs in convoluted meanderings. High red sandstone cliffs loomed on the horizon in all directions, and a great flat ledge called The White Rim formed a strange level boundary between the high red sandstone cliffs above and the softer reddish mudstone cliffs that dropped off into the deep canyon of the sluggish Green River. Adventuresome uranium prospectors had punched a jeep trail up from the Colorado River near Moab onto the level White Rim, so that a high clearance four-wheel drive vehicle could navigate along the lip of the White Rim around the heads of the side canyons clear from the Colorado River to overlooks into the canyon of the Green River. It was impossible to drive down into the Green River Canyon itself.

Finally, out beyond majestic Grandview Point and the isolated high mesa called Island in the Sky, the greenish waters of the Green River met with the reddish muddy waters of the Colorado River in a deep inaccessible canyon. For almost two miles the green and red waters flowed along side each other, gradually merging into a single muddy current. The Colorado flowed off at an angle toward the southwest into Cataract Canyon and eventually into Glen Canyon, while their route of flight bore them just east of due south across a stark terrain of numerous thin sandstone ridges called Fins, separating narrow straight sandy slots or valleys, all running parallel toward the southwest.

Clay recognized these bizarre erosional features as something produced by a parallel joint system in the overlying sandstone formation, but to the untrained eye it looked like something that God had created in a whimsical moment. It was a trackless wilderness, probably seldom traveled by mankind, but certainly impassable to modern vehicles. This was the fabled Needles Area where cattle had been released to graze but never came back out. Clay wondered if some cowboys sent in after the cattle had met the same fate.

Ahead loomed the northern flanks of 9,000-foot Elk Ridge and 11,000-foot Abajo Peak could be seen just to the east of their southerly course. The transition from the incredible maze of the Needles Area to the snowy heights of Elk Ridge was the most awesome terrain Clay had ever seen, and it could be seen best from a low flying airplane.

Sweeping down across the snow drifted rolling expanse of Elk Ridge and its isolated patches of tall pines, Clay saw no evidence of any vehicle traffic on the roads, but big game tracks were everywhere. The solid snow cover of early April was just beginning to melt and bare patches of the dirt roads and sage covered flats showed through. Windrows of drifted snow and gullies filled with wind drifted snow were everywhere. Clay spotted where he and Jerry had driven up the road from Blanding far to the east, and then turned around. He could tell that no one had driven the road since and he was surprised.

Up ahead the roof tops of Bluff were shining in the morning sun and off to the southwest were the buttes and spires of Monument Valley, majestic in their presence looming in the surrounding emptiness. The Navajo reservation is mostly an empty arid sandstone expanse dotted with dirt covered Navajo hogans which are invisible from above unless marked by a parked pickup truck.

Off to the east was the landmark of the Navajo reservation, mighty Ship Rock, a volcanic cluster of spires resembling a three-masted schooner in the flat expanse of empty desert. Further to the southeast was the 9,000-foot Chuska Mountain Range, sacred to the Navajos. Canyon De Chelly was beneath them, but from the air the cliff dwellings nestled under the sandstone cliffs were invisible. Numerous dirt roads on the dry canyon floor told Clay this was a much visited place. Soon after passing Canyon De Chelly, Jim reduced engine power slightly and started his long descent to the Window Rock airstrip.

Leveling off and starting to circle the airstrip, Jim turned to Clay. "What time is your appointment with the tribal leaders?"

"1:30 PM," Clay answered.

"We're mighty early, and there isn't any place to eat here," Jim replied. "I suggest we fly to Gallup and grab a bite of lunch at the air terminal there. I can get you back to Window Rock in plenty of time to make your meeting. How do you plan to get to the offices?"

"Hell, I don't even know where they are," Clay said, laughing.

Within minutes Jim was circling the Gallup airport, preparing to land. As he touched down and the plane rolled down the paved runway, Clay noticed two identical twin-engined Beechcraft airplanes emblazoned with Navajo Nation parked on the ramp. Jim quickly taxied up to the fueling island and shut down the engine. An Indian man in bright red coveralls came over to meet them and asked what kind of fuel they wanted. Jim specified 80-octane, both tanks.

"Are you familiar with the airstrip at Window Rock?" Jim asked the man as he dragged a long hose to the fuel cap on the left wing.

"Nah, but the guy in the office can help you," he replied, pointing to a small white shack beyond the tie-down area. While Jim supervised the fueling,

Clay walked over and was told that a tribal police vehicle met all flights landing at the Window Rock airstrip and could take him to his appointment. Very convenient, Clay thought.

Clay and Jim ordered a cold soft drink and a hamburger with fries, standard fare at the lunch counter in the air terminal. Jim cautioned Clay to sample the catsup before he doused his hamburger. It was labeled "mildly nippy" but was highly spiced for the local trade and tasted like Tabasco Sauce. Clay was grateful for the warning.

Clay sat at the counter for a few minutes organizing his thoughts for his meeting, while Jim went outside. At 12:30 Jim returned and they flew the 20 miles to Window Rock where Jim buzzed the main street, "To wake up the tribal police" he said to Clay. By the time Jim was lined up on his final approach for landing Clay spotted a white sedan driving up to the airstrip. Jim touched down lightly on the gravel airstrip and taxied up to the parked police car.

"I'll fly back to Gallup to wait," Jim said, "but I'll return within two hours unless you telephone me to come earlier. Don't lose that telephone number I gave you."

As Clay headed toward the car, Jim gunned the engine and was off.

The Navajo police sergeant was very cordial when he learned that Clay had an appointment with the president at tribal headquarters. He handed Clay a card with his telephone number so Clay could call him for a ride back to the airstrip. He then drove Clay to the entrance of a modern building with a large sign out front reading Navajo Nation. Clay thanked him, entered the spacious entry foyer and walked up to an impressive counter manned by two Navajo women. He identified himself and was quickly escorted to a large paneled office where another elegantly dressed Navajo woman was the receptionist. She asked him to have a seat in a large soft easy chair behind a low coffee table covered with magazines.

A few minutes past 1:30 the receptionist received a call and asked Clay to follow her down a long hall. She opened a frosted glass paneled door and ushered Clay into a large conference room where four well dressed Navajo men were seated at the far end of a large conference table scattered with papers.

The man at the end of the table stood up. "Come in Mr. Greer. I am Peter Begay, and this is Walter Tsagi my attorney general. This is John Oraibi in charge of mineral resources, and Pablo Dinah our treasurer. Please be seated and tell us why you've come."

Clay noticed that each man was well dressed in snappy western styled suits, and each wore the largest silver and turquoise bolo ties he had ever seen. Mr. Begay and the attorney also wore the largest silver and turquoise belt buckles he had ever seen outside the winner's circle at a rodeo. Begay's belt buckle was at least eight inches in diameter and must weigh a pound, Clay thought to himself.

Clay quickly reached into his portfolio and handed each of the men his business card, and then placed his notes before him on the polished table. It gave him a moment to gather his senses in such intimidating surroundings. Hoping his voice wouldn't crack from nervous tension, he identified himself as a consulting geologist from Salt Lake City. He explained that he represented a client, whose identity he was not at liberty to reveal, who was interested in exploring the Navajo reservation for minerals, not including oil or gas or coal. He stated that his client wished to obtain an exclusive exploration concession for an area in the northern portion of the reservation for starters. He further stated that his client wanted to work out a long term mining lease in advance, contingent upon a successful out-come of their exploration efforts. The royalty rate, any annual rental or minimum royalty, and yearly work requirements were critical elements that must be decided before exploration expenses could be incurred, he explained.

"Exactly what specific minerals will be sought?" Mr. Oraibi asked.

"All kinds of minerals, metals, non-metallics, industrial minerals, precious and semi-precious stones, everything except oil and gas, and coal deposits, as I said," Clay replied.

"How much are you willing to pay for this exploration concession?" Mr. Dinah asked.

"Well, since we are willing to use our own capital searching for mineral deposits which, if found, will yield substantial revenues to the tribe and create employment for tribal members, we had hoped the cash outlay for the concession would be minimal, at least for the first year," Clay replied.

"How large an area are you interested in?" said the attorney, Mr. Tsagi. "And will you be exploring for uranium?"

Clay paused for a moment. "Our immediate interest is in the Aneth Area, along Montezuma Creek and its tributaries. That would include the McCracken Mesa area the tribe is scheduled to acquire soon. We'll need several thousand acres to do a complete exploration project, but perhaps only a few hundred acres for a mining lease once we identify a mineral deposit. As for uranium deposits, yes, we would expect to explore for uranium, but if uranium poses a problem, we could exclude it."

"How can we be assured that your project won't interfere with our residents, and the companies we have already given mineral leases to?" Mr. Begay asked. "I mean, of course, oil and gas leases. We haven't given any coal leases in the Aneth area, have we John?" Oraibi shook his head.

"I assure you, gentlemen," Clay said, "any exploration concession we propose will not endanger residents of the area or any current lessees."

"Mr. Greer," Mr. Oraibi said, taking the lead. "The long standing practice of the Navajo Nation has been that we will not enter into any negotiations or leases until we have identified and approved the parties with whom we are dealing. The tribe doesn't enter into arrangements with parties unwilling to expose themselves to our scrutiny. Second, the tribe doesn't grant exploration concessions, which are in effect hunting licenses for mineral deposits. Third, if we consider granting your client a lease it will be only for mining a specified mineral or commodity. In other words, if you propose to look for, say, gold, we might issue you a lease for gold, for a maximum term of ten years, during which time you can explore for gold and mine any gold you find. But if you were to discover a silver deposit, or a copper deposit, you would have no rights to those deposits. Those deposits would belong to the tribe. Of course, after the ten-year term of your lease, even the gold deposit would revert to us. Therefore, if you will name the specific mineral or commodity you are searching for, and if you are prepared to disclose the identity of your client, then we'll be prepared to negotiate with you as your client's authorized agent. The tribe cannot accept your proposal for an exploration concession."

Clay stared at them for a moment. "Mr. Oraibi, I think I understand what you're saying." He paused for effect, then continued in a soft voice, "You understand that my client is willing to spend a considerable amount of money to explore for mineral deposits which no one presently knows even exist. If we find nothing, it will have cost my client a lot, but it will have cost the tribe nothing. However, if we find something, anything, of value, then both my client and the tribe will benefit. Unless my client is allowed to explore, any new mineral deposits may never be found. Please give my proposal your thoughtful consideration."

No one spoke for a few minutes. Mr. Begay broke the silence. "Mr. Greer, will you give us a few minutes while we discuss your proposal further?"

"Of course," Clay said, gathering up his papers. In the reception area he nervously sank into a soft chair to await their decision.

After about thirty minutes the receptionist's telephone buzzed and she motioned for Clay to re-enter the conference room. Begay and Oraibi were the only ones still at the conference table.

Begay motioned for Clay to take his seat. "Mr. Greer, the tribe is unwilling to alter its practices for your client. I suggest you go back and explain our procedures for leasing minerals on the reservation. When your client is ready to comply, call my secretary for another appointment. I hope I will hear from you again. Good day." Then the two got up and left by a private door.

Clay sat at the empty conference table for a moment, then headed for the receptionist's desk. He asked permission to call number in Gallup, and then the tribal police for a ride back to the airstrip.

In only a few minutes the police car arrived and he was soon back at the airstrip, waiting for Jim. He was seething with anger at his inability to negotiate with the tribal officers and could see the project collapsing. He was glad to be leaving the Tribal headquarters, even if it was empty handed. He wanted to get back to Blanding and Hatch Trading Post as fast as he could.

Jim's silver Cessna 180 circled the field and glided in for a smooth landing. Clay waved as Jim taxied up and climbed into the airplane while the engine was still turning. "Let's get the hell out of this place," Clay shouted into Jim's ear over the engine noise. Jim frowned. "Things didn't go so well, huh?" Clay nodded and remained silent during the takeoff.

As Window Rock disappeared behind the climbing airplane, Clay began to unwind as he looked out at the impressive view unfolding beneath him. Golly, Clay thought to himself, if Jerry's fossil mine can make us the money he thinks it can, I'm gonna buy me an airplane with my share.

The flight back to Blanding would take only 50 minutes, so Clay would arrive about 3:30, about a half hour before Jerry was scheduled to meet him. That was pretty good planning. At least something about this hasty trip was working out.

Before long Clay spotted the pillars of Monument Valley off to the northwest, then Bluff ahead on north bank of the San Juan. Jim reduced power for the long descent, reducing the noise in the plane.

"Sounds like the Navajo leadership gave you the treatment," Jim said. into Clay's left ear. "Were they insulting, or just disappointing?"

"Some of both," Clay responded, able to talk about his encounter now. "Basically, they wanted everything in the way of disclosure and weren't about to commit anything in return. How in the devil do those guys ever do any business with that attitude? How did those oil companies ever get their leases at Aneth?"

Jim shook his head. "I can't say for sure, but I'll bet the oil companies just smothered the tribal leaders in cash, and now hope to make it back out of production. Clay, it's like you have been told, if the Navajo bosses aren't awed by you, they probably won't deal with you. At least, that's what I've been told and I believe it."

The Blanding airfield was now in sight and Clay looked at his watch. It was 3:35 and Jerry's pickup truck wasn't anywhere on the field. If fact, the airfield was completely empty of vehicles, even parked airplanes.

Jim lined up with the runway on his final approach for a landing to the south and the Cessna glided down, its wheels touching down right on the large numbers painted on the asphalt. As they taxied Jim turned to Clay. "You want me to wait with you until Jerry arrives? I've still got plenty of time to make Green River in the daylight."

Clay thanked him but pointed out that he could call Charlie Nevilles to come for him if Jerry didn't show up by dark. While the engine was still running Clay climbed out and waved goodbye. Pulling the right side door snuggly closed, Jim added power and taxied back out onto the runway and back down to the north end. As Clay watched in admiration, Jim cycled the prop, checked the mags, spun around in a tight circle to check for any landing traffic, then lined up on the centerline of the runway and added full power. The lightly loaded Cessna 180 practically leapt into the air, banked and climbed steeply toward the north. In a few minutes the small shining object disappeared into the sky over Elk Ridge, headed in a beeline for Green River.

Clay stared after the plane for a few minutes, now more determined than ever to buy his own if Jerry's prediction of financial success in the fossil mining business came true. Clay was suddenly brought back to reality as a familiar pickup rattled across the cattleguard at the entrance into the fenced airport, and a grinning Jerry Brooks braked to a halt beside him. Clay opened the door and climbed in.

"When I saw Jim's airplane I knew you had just arrived. Man, I call that good timing. How did the negotiations go?" Jerry said. Then he took a look at his friend's face. "Say no more, your grim look tells me everything."

Clay spilled out his disappointment and frustration, detailing every aspect of his meeting and the cold reception he received. "They left the door open for me to come back," Clay added, "but I think Mr. George will drop this project like a hot potato. What do you think we should do? How are we going to continue to mine fossils once the Navajos take over McCracken Mesa?"

"I had lots of time, driving down by myself, to think on that subject," Jerry said, "and I sort of anticipated your negotiations might not pan out. I have an idea I'd like to run by you tonight while I fix supper. Don't feel bad about your negotiations not working out. Mr. George saw the writing on the wall pretty early, while our optimism blinded us. You really counted on tearing up the whole countryside looking for diamonds, but now we'll just have to live with our secret discovery and its unrealized potential."

The lights of Hatch Trading Post soon appeared in the dusk through the cottonwood trees ahead and Clay found himself looking forward to Jerry's gourmet cooking and a discussion of Jerry's Plan.

13

JERRY'S PLAN

After Clay and Jerry opened up their tent, unrolled their bedrolls and fired up the camp stove, the place took on a homey atmosphere. Jerry had purchased some steaks on the drive down and soon had them cooking on a large aluminum griddle. Canned vegetables rounded out the meal. Clay readied the eating utensils and fished cold pop from the ice filled cooler in the pickup. The gasoline lanterns added a bright, cheery feeling to the camp as they sat down to eat.

"Tell me this plan you've worked out," Clay said between bites. "I'm mighty curious."

Jerry gathered his thoughts. "Driving back to Blanding I got to thinking. What if Clay gets turned down by the tribe, what could we do then? I'm not gonna just walk away from this gold mine we've found in Alkali Wash. I figure that until the BLM formally declares the mining claims invalid, like that fellow Hu Norris said, we can continue operating without interruption. I suggest we really speed things up and get the most valuable material out of the ground and stockpiled off Indian land. Nevilles' storage yard is perfect for now. Eventually, when the BLM kicks us off, I think Peter Shonto and his crew could continue to mine. They are Navajos and this is a Navajo reservation. BLM won't have any say. I've taught Pete and his crew well, and they like the work. They stand to make a lot of money selling the material to me. I don't figure the tribe will throw Navajo workers off a deposit they're operating themselves.

"Sure sounds logical to me. You've really figured this out, Jerry. How much do you figure we can get out of this deposit?"

Jerry smiled. "I'll bet your net share ought to be around $100,000, maybe a lot more."

"Well, that sure makes me feel better," Clay replied, "In fact, flying back from Window Rock I made up my mind to buy an airplane and reactivate my pilot's license. This makes it possible. I love flying and it sure makes sense to travel by private plane in my business."

The next morning Clay was the first one out of the tent. "Where the Hell is my Jeep?" Clay shouted, rushing back into the tent.

Jerry sat up, rubbed his eyes and laughed. "Shonto and his workers drove it up to the mine. He's been doing that while we were in Salt Lake, remember?"

"Oh," Clay stammered, settling down. "I guess I forgot."

So they quickly ate breakfast and headed there themselves. Pete Shonto walked over to meet them as they drove up.

"Look at this," he said, pointing to the ground near the fossil stream channel. "We didn't want to touch this until you returned." A complete dinosaur skeleton lay in the mudstone, apparently right where it had died 160 million years ago.

"Wow, let me get my camera," Jerry said, going back to his truck. "I need to document where each piece lies before we disturbed anything. We'll want to identify and number the separate parts, so the skeleton can be reassembled again. A complete dinosaur skeleton ought to be quite valuable, so we need to be real careful." He turned to Clay. "Just think, if we hadn't come along and dug this while it's still intact, erosion would have exposed it in a few years and washed it down the gully. Just so many scraps of dinosaur bone of little value to paleontologists. Some museum will be delighted to get this skeleton. Wow, what a find!"

During their lunch break Jerry laid out his plan to Peter Shonto. He in turn discussed it with the workers and they all accepted it. Clay and Jerry felt relieved at this response.

"Oh, I nearly forgot," Peter said after lunch. "Bud Menlove and his partner dropped by while you were in Salt Lake. They wanted to thank you for the first royalty payment, and they looked over our operation. They checked to see how we weighed the fossil materials and seemed to be satisfied with the way we are doing things."

Jerry and Clay were pleased with Pete Shonto's orderly work as they walked around later. Everything was being handled efficiently. Several large wooden boxes were brimming with agatized dinosaur bone. Imprints in the dirt indicated that other boxes had been hauled away to Blanding. Dinosaur bones and large fragments of bones, some well agatized, lay in several piles ready for transport. Off to the side were several mounds of gravel that needed to be run through the rocker. It didn't look like any gravel had been washed and that was fine with Clay. Secretly he still hoped to discover another pocket of diamonds to impress Mr. George. The true mining prospector is eternally optimistic.

Clay noticed that Pete was using the front mounted power winch on his Jeep to drag very large petrified wood logs from the fossil channel over to one of the stockpiles. Pretty inventive, he thought, and certainly the most use the winch had seen since it was installed in 1954. Clay could only recall using the winch about a dozen times to get unstuck or to navigate over steep ledges.

About this time Smiley Kerr drove up. As Clay and Jerry approached, he said, "Mr. Nevilles wants you to come by his place. I think he's running out of storage for your stuff."

"When I was in Salt Lake," Jerry said on the way to Blanding, "I talked to a neighbor near my shop about leasing a large fenced area. Then when I drove through Monticello, I stopped in to talk to the uranium trucking firm next to the AEC ore buying station. You know, where all those really big hauling trucks are parked. Well, it turns out the trucker takes his equipment to Salt Lake for heavy maintenance and repairs, and for only four cents a ton-mile he'll come down to Blanding, load up, and haul to any destination in Salt Lake. He even offered to back-haul any supplies from Salt Lake to Monticello, for us to pick up there, for free. One of his big trucks, fully loaded, could handle nearly a week's worth of production at the mine. He sends about one truck a week to Salt Lake now. We ought to get him started hauling out of Nevilles' yard now."

"Good planning, Jerry," Clay said.

Charlie was relieved to learn about their plans. Clay understood why when he saw how much material was piled up inside Charlie's fenced yard. He quietly walked among the boxes of agate and neat piles of fossil wood and dinosaur bone, mentally calculating the resale value.

I can see that plane is clearly in my future, he thought to himself.

Clay telephoned Mr. George in Los Angeles to report the disappointing meeting with the Navajo leaders. As Clay had anticipated, he decided to terminate the venture as of the end of the month and asked Clay to send him the bills. Clay offered to cut off all expenses to the investors immediately and deliver the gemstones, including diamonds from the unwashed gravels at the mine. Mr. George then suggested that Clay keep a few of the diamonds as mementos of his successful search for the source of the gemstones, even if it had turned out to be less than commercially viable. Mr. George still couldn't bring himself to use the word diamonds, Clay realized.

In the next few days back at the mine, Clay and his team of workers succeeded in washing and panning the accumulated gravel. They recovered four good sized diamonds and a lot of smaller fragments which Clay carefully put in glass vials and sent to Mr. George, along with a final billing for the investors' share of expenses.

About a week later when work settled into a routine, Clay spent one evening lamping the deposit for diamonds. He was excited to find a small pocket of respectable sized stones which he and Jerry carefully dug out. Clay divided the cache into equal thirds, sending one third to Mr. George as a bonus. It made them feel that everything was now even.

Jerry kept very busy over the next week managing their mining empire, supervising Pete and the Navajo workers at the fossil mine, monitoring Smiley's trucking schedule and the growing stockpile at Blanding, and arranging for periodic haul trips to Salt Lake City. Their business there was booming. Mary had even contacted some big dealers in California and Arizona who wanted to take delivery of their orders at Blanding to save a lot of unnecessary hauling. Jerry trained Nancy Nevilles to take orders over her telephone and send messages via Smiley to Jerry, or Clay, at Hatch.

Clay, with some time on his hands, actively prospected the other fossil river channels at night with ultraviolet lamps. To his amazement he found another pocket of diamonds in one channel and this only teased him to keep looking. The presence of alluvial diamonds in these 160 million year old river channels was too good to just walk away from, but not good enough to expend more money to pursue. The worldwide mining experience was filled with similar quandaries.

Jerry sometimes accompanied Clay on these nighttime prospecting forays, though he could ill afford the time. He had come to the conclusion that he and the Navajos could never exhaust all the deposits of petrified wood and dinosaur bone in these fossil stream channels. He came to reluctantly realize that closing the reservation to future fossil mining was the only way to prevent flooding the market, at least at the prices the rock buying market was currently willing to pay. Somehow, that realization sweetened an otherwise bitter situation.

As time passed, and their profitable fossil mining and marketing venture began to pay off, Clay made a down payment on a new Cessna 182, a tricycle landing gear version of Jim Hewitt's venerable Cessna 180. It had the same engine, wings and stout fuselage as the Cessna 180, but it had a nose wheel, rather than the old fashioned tail wheel, which made for better visibility during taxi and more positive ground handling on landing and takeoff.

Jim Hewitt winced when he heard about Clay's choice of this new landing gear configuration, remarking that the nose wheel would surely crumple and collapse on rough dirt landing strips. But Clay's flight instructor at Thompson Flying Service in Salt Lake City, where Clay had bought the Cessna 182, showed him how you hold the control yoke back tightly in your lap during the initial takeoff run, or just as the airplane touched down on landing, and avoid nose-wheel contact with the ground altogether. Flown correctly, the Cessna 182 was as durable on rough airstrips as the classic Cessna 180. As Clay's instructor phrased it, "The new Cessna 182 is a Cessna 180 with manners."

The flight from Salt Lake to Blanding now took less than two hours. Clay never felt comfortable flying over the trackless Needles Area south of the confluence of the Green River and the Colorado, so he generally detoured via Moab and Monticello, lengthening the time to an even two hours.

Jerry liked Clay's new toy, but refused to fly when the weather was turbulent or stormy. "This is a fair weather machine," he always said, and Clay tended to agree.

And when his busy scheduled allowed, Clay often flew to Denver where he had started courting pretty Sandy Logan.

In time the BLM mining claim inspectors issued their formal report, and the owners of the Yellow Bird claims were served with a complaint challenging the validity of their mining claims in Alkali Wash. Clay and Jerry urged Bud Menlove and Jack Glover to defend their mining claims. But Menlove and Glover had other things to spend their money on and said Clay and Jerry could respond to the legal action if they wanted to but as claim owners, they weren't going to try.

Jerry recommended they slip immediately into the Shonto Mining Mode, as he phrased it. Clay agreed.

The fossil mine at Alkali Wash now became an exclusive Indian operation supervised by Peter Shonto, and Jerry closed their camp at Hatch Trading Post. The tent, cooking fly, camp stove and lanterns, and all the camping gear rented from Charlie Nevilles were returned, with much thanks for its use. By now Nancy Nevilles was running an efficient branch operation of Jerry's rock shop, writing up the frequent sales to buyers who drove their trucks and vans in from California, Arizona and Colorado. She was paid a sales commission and for a while was making so much money she began to tease Charlie, that she was the family breadwinner now.

In October of 1957 the Atomic Energy Commission formally announced termination of its Uranium Ore Buying Program, and imposed an allocation on all producing uranium mines for future ore purchases. New or undeveloped uranium deposits, with no AEC ore allocation, simply had no guaranteed government market for their uranium ores. The results for the uranium mining industry weren't exactly what some had so confidently predicted, especially after President Eisenhower released to civilian power utilities a billion dollars' worth of enriched uranium from AEC stockpiles at subsidized prices.

The predicted civilian scramble for uranium ore reserves didn't materialize. Producing uranium mines, put on a government allocation diet, weren't in the mood for expansion; new uranium prospects without an allocation had absolutely no market for their uranium ores, and couldn't raise a dime for needed capital costs to get into production. All the general public prospectors, whom the AEC had so vigorously recruited to come to the desolate Colorado Plateau, quietly went home. The speculative market for uranium mining company shares dried up overnight, and when that happened the professional mining promoters simply shifted into other promising businesses like selling desert lands for retirement communities or speculating in Las Vegas land developments. The stockbrokers who couldn't unload uranium shares any longer started touting the shares of emerging local oil companies, or other non-uranium mining ventures.

The once bustling southeastern Utah uranium boomtowns like Moab, Monticello and Green River, went into temporary decline, and outlying settlements back in the isolated canyons simply dried up. Grand Junction, Colorado, the Capital of the Uranium Boom, took a hit when the market price for uranium nosedived and the prospectors left the region. Empty ramshackle house trailers and shacks dotted the empty canyons where aspiring small uranium mines had once prospered. Untended mine portals in the multi-colored Morrison formation and waste dumps of pastel colored mud and rocks were all that remained of once bustling uranium ventures in this desert region. What had only a few years ago been an empty, uninhabited labyrinth of deep canyons and colorful plateaus, quickly returned to its former state. In the scattered local communities a few oldtimers stubbornly hung on, convinced that the uranium industry would revive, or something else would come along to replace the vanished prosperity.

Far to the south of the uranium belt, on the Navajo reservation, oil companies were finding and developing huge oil and natural gas fields in the very Mesozoic formations from which uranium had been produced in the 1950s. Development of these fields was extending gradually north into western Colorado and eastern Utah, and commercial development of deep potash deposits near Moab continued to progress.

Clayton P. Greer was in the front ranks of the experts who consulted on geological matters with the new oil companies and aspiring potash developers flooding into the region. In a sense, the oldtimers were right.

POSTSCRIPT

One day in late March of 1958 Clay Greer got a call at his office from Blaine Issac George. Mr. George would be in Salt Lake City on business, and he invited Clay to lunch at the Rooftop Restaurant of the Newhouse Hotel. Clay was surprised and pleased to hear from his old client, and they arranged a time and date.

On the appointed day Clay walked over from his office to the hotel, took the elevator to the top floor, and upon entering the restaurant spotted a familiar large gray haired gentleman sitting at a table with another well dressed man about 60 years old. Mr. George got up and greeted Clay as he walked in.

Turning to his companion, Mr. George said, "See, Paul, this is the Clay Greer I've told you so much about." Paul smiled and extended his hand as Mr. George continued, "Clay, this is my good friend Paul, from Los Angeles. He was one of my California investors in the gemstone project last year. Paul is in the oil business, and when he asked me about the booming oil activity in Utah, I promised to introduce him to you." Turning back to Paul, he said, "Clay was completely dedicated and fair in all of his dealings with me. He is a very knowledgeable geologist. I couldn't recommend anyone to you more highly."

Clay and Paul looked at each other in the pause that followed, and Clay noticed that Paul wore a large marquise-cut faceted diamond in a custom designed bolo tie. It looked elegant. "Is that one of the stones we recovered for Mr. George?" Clay said, pointing.

Paul fingered the bolo instinctively, smiled and nodded. Clay continued, "Paul, tell me about your interest in oil exploration in Utah. But first, tell me your full name. I didn't get that."

Paul looked surprised, glanced at Mr. George, then back to Clay, and replied, "I'm J. Paul Getty. I thought you knew . . . ."

Printed in the United States
5200

9 780865 343474